Dax's Gaze Drifted Lower And Focused On Elise's Mouth.

Because he was thinking about kissing her. She could read it all over his expression.

Emergency. This wasn't a date. She'd led him on somehow. They didn't like each other, and worse, he shied away from everything she desired—love, marriage, soul mates. She was supposed to be matching him with one of her clients.

First and foremost, she'd given him permission to ruin her business if he didn't find the love of his life. And she was compromising the entire thing.

Had she lost her mind?

Despite knowing he thought happily ever after was a myth, despite knowing he faked interest in her as a method of distraction, despite knowing he stood to lose five hundred thousand dollars and pretended to misunderstand her questions or refused to answer them strictly to prevent it—despite all that, she'd wanted him to kiss her.

Dax Wakefield was better at seducing a woman than she'd credited.

Matched
to Her Rival

KAT CANTRELL

First published in Great Britain 2014
by Mills & Boon, an imprint of Harlequin (UK) Limited,
Large Print edition 2014
Eton House, 18-24 Paradise Road,
Richmond, Surrey, TW9 1SR

© 2014 Kat Cantrell

ISBN: 978-0-263-24437-3

Harlequin (UK) Limited's policy is to use papers that are natural, renewable and recyclable products and made from wood grown in sustainable forests. The logging and manufacturing processes conform to the legal environmental regulations of the country of origin.

Printed and bound in Great Britain
by CPI Antony Rowe, Chippenham, Wiltshire

KAT CANTRELL

read her first Mills & Boon® novel in third grade and has been scribbling in notebooks since she learned to spell. What else would she write but romance? She majored in literature, officially with the intent to teach, but somehow ended up buried in middle management in corporate America, until she became a stay-at-home mum and full-time writer.

Kat, her husband and their two boys live in north Texas. When she's not writing about characters on the journey to happily-ever-after, she can be found at a soccer game, watching the TV show *Friends* or listening to '80s music.

Kat was the 2011 Harlequin So You Think You Can Write winner and a 2012 RWA Golden Heart finalist for best unpublished series contemporary manuscript.

To Jill Marsal, agent extraordinaire,
because you stuck with me
through all the revisions of this book
and together, we made it great.
And because this one was
your favorite of the three.

One

In the media business—and in life—presentation trumped everything else, and Dax Wakefield never underestimated the value of putting on a good show.

Careful attention to every detail was the reason his far-flung media empire had succeeded beyond his wildest dreams. So why was KDLS, the former jewel of his crown, turning in such dismal ratings?

Dax stopped at the receptionist's desk in the lobby of the news station he'd come to fix. "Hey, Rebecca. How's Brian's math grade this semester?"

The receptionist's smile widened as she fluffed

her hair and threw her shoulders back to make sure he noticed her impressive figure.

He noticed. A man who enjoyed the female form as much as Dax always noticed.

"Good morning, Mr. Wakefield," Rebecca chirped. "He made a C on his last report card. Such an improvement. It's been like six months since I mentioned his grades. How on earth did you remember?"

Because Dax made it a point to keep at least one personal detail about all his employees front and center when speaking to them. The mark of success wasn't simply who had the most money, but who had the best-run business, and no one could do it all by themselves. If people liked working for you, they stuck around, and turned themselves inside out to perform.

Usually. Dax had a few questions for Robert Smith, the station manager, about the latest ratings. Someone was tripping up somewhere.

Dax tapped his temple and grinned. "My mama encourages me to use this bad boy for good instead of evil. Is Robert around?"

The receptionist nodded and buzzed the lock on the security door. "They're taping a segment. I'm sure he's hovering near the set."

"Say hi to Brian for me," Dax called as he sailed through the frosted glass door and into the greatest show on earth—the morning news.

Cameramen and gaffers mixed it up, harried producers with electronic tablets stepped over thick cables on their way to the sound booth, and in the middle of it all sat KDLS's star anchor, Monica McCreary. She was conversing on camera with a petite dark-haired woman who had great legs, despite being on the shorter side. She'd done a lot with what she had and he appreciated the effort.

Dax paused at the edge of the organized chaos and crossed his arms, locking gazes with the station manager. With a nod, Robert scurried across the ocean of people and equipment to join him.

"Saw the ratings, huh?" Robert murmured.

That was a quality Dax fully appreciated in his employees—the ability to read his mind.

Low ratings irritated him because there was no excuse. Sensationalism was key, and if nothing newsworthy happened, it was their job to create something worth watching, and ensure that something had Wakefield Media stamped on it.

"Yep." Dax left it at that, for now. He had all day and the crew was in the middle of taping. "What's this segment?"

"Dallas business owners. We feature one a week. Local interest stuff."

Great Legs owned her own business? Interesting. Smart women equaled a huge turn-on.

"What's she do? Cupcakes?"

Even from this distance, the woman exuded energy—a perky little cheerleader type who never met a curlicue or excess of decoration she didn't like. He could see her dolloping frosting on a cupcake and charging an exorbitant price for it.

Dax could go for a cupcake. Literally and figuratively. Maybe even at the same time.

"Nah. She runs a dating service." Robert nodded at the pair of women under the spotlight. "EA International. Caters to exclusive clients."

The back of Dax's neck heated instantly and all thoughts of cupcakes went out the window.

"I'm familiar with the company."

Through narrowed eyes, Dax zeroed in on the Dallas business owner who had cost him his oldest friend. Someone who called herself a matchmaker should be withered and stooped, with gray hair. It was such an antiquated notion. And it should be against the law.

The anchor laughed at something the matchmaker said and leaned forward. "So you're Dallas's answer to a fairy godmother?"

"I like to think of myself as one. Who doesn't need a bit of magic in their lives?" Her sleek dark hair swung freely as she talked with her hands, expression animated.

"You recently matched the Delamerian prince with his fiancée, right?" Monica winked. "Women everywhere are cursing that, I'm sure."

"I can't take credit." The matchmaker smiled and it transformed her entire demeanor. "Prince Alain—Finn—and Juliet had a previous relationship. I just helped them realize it wasn't over."

Dax couldn't stop watching her.

As much as he hated to admit it, the matchmaker lit up the set. KDLS's star news anchor was more of a minor celestial body compared to the matchmaker's sun.

And Dax was never one to underestimate star power.

Or the element of surprise.

He strode onto the set and dismissed the anchor with a jerk of his head. "I'll take over from here, Monica. Thanks."

Despite the unusual request, Monica smiled and vacated her chair without comment. No one else so much as blinked. No one who worked for him, anyway.

As he parked in Monica's still-warm chair, the petite dynamo opposite him nearly bowled him over when she blurted out, "What's going on? Who are you?"

A man who recognized a golden opportunity for improved ratings.

"Dax Wakefield. I own the station," he said smoothly. "And this interview has officially started over. It's Elise, right?"

Her confusion leveled out and she crossed her spectacular legs, easing back in the chair carefully. "Yes, but you can call me Ms. Arundel."

Ah, so she recognized his name. Let the fun begin.

He chuckled darkly. "How about if I call you Ms. Hocus-Pocus instead? Isn't that your gig, pulling fast ones on unsuspecting clients? You bibbidi-bobbidi-boo women into relationships with wealthy men."

This interview had also officially become the best way to dish up a side of revenge—served cold. If this ratings gold mine led to discrediting EA International, so much the better. Someone had to save the world from this matchmaker's mercenary female clients.

"That's not what I do." Elise's gaze cut from his face to his torso and her expression did not melt into the typical sensuous smile that said she'd be happy to further discuss whatever he wanted to talk about over drinks. Unlike most women.

It whetted his appetite to get sparks on the screen another way.

"Enlighten us then," he allowed magnanimously with a wave of his hand.

"I match soul mates." Elise, pardon-me-Ms.-Arundel, cleared her throat and recrossed her legs as if she couldn't find a comfortable pose. "Some people need more help than others. Successful men seldom have time or the patience to sort through potential love interests. I do it for them. At the same time, a man with means needs a certain kind of mate, one not easily found. I widen the potential pool by polishing a few of my female clients into diamonds worthy of the highest social circles."

"Oh, come now. You're training these women to be gold diggers."

That was certainly what she'd done with Daniella White, whose last name was now Reynolds because she'd managed to snare Dax's college friend Leo. Who then promptly screwed Dax over in favor of his wife. A fifteen-year friendship down the drain. Over a woman.

Elise's smile hardened. "You're suggesting women need a class on how to marry a man for his money? I doubt anyone with that goal needs help honing her strategy. I'm in the business of making women's lives better by introducing them to their soul mates."

"Why not pay for them to go to college and let them find their own dates?" Dax countered swiftly.

The onlookers shifted and murmured but neither Dax nor Elise so much as glanced away from their staring contest. An indefinable crackle sliced through the air between them. It was going to be beautiful on camera.

"There are scholarship opportunities out there already. I'm filling another niche, helping people connect. I'm good at what I do. You of all people should know that."

Oh, she had not just gone there. Nearly nose to nose now, he smiled, the best method to keep 'em guessing. "Why would I know that? Because you single-handedly ruined both a business venture and a long-standing friendship when you introduced Leo to his gold digger?"

So, apparently that wound was still raw.

College roommates who'd seen the world through the same lens, he and Leo believed wholeheartedly in the power of success and brotherhood. Females were to be appreciated until they outlived their usefulness. Until Daniella, who somehow got Leo to fall in love with her and then she'd brainwashed his oldest friend into losing his ruthless business edge.

Not that he believed Daniella was 100 percent at fault. She'd been the instigator but Leo had pulled the plug on the deal with Dax. Both he and Leo had suffered a seven-figure loss. Then Leo ended their friendship for no reason.

The pain of his friend's betrayal still had the power to punch quite a hole through his stomach. That was why it never paid to trust people. Anyone you let in eventually stomped all over you.

"No!" She huffed a sigh of frustration and shut her eyes for a beat, clearly trying to come up with a snappy response. Good luck with that. There wasn't one.

But she tried anyway. "Because I single-handedly helped two people find each other and fall in love. Something real and lasting happened before your eyes and you had a front-row seat. Leo and Dannie are remarkably compatible and share values. That's what my computer does. Matches people according to who they are."

"The magic you alluded to earlier," Dax commented with raised eyebrows. "Right? It's all smoke and mirrors, though. You tell these people they're compatible and they fall for it. The power of suggestion. Quite brilliant, actually."

And he meant it. If anyone knew the benefit of smoke and mirrors, he did. It kept everyone distracted from what was really going on behind the curtain, where the mess was.

A red stain spilled across Elise's cheeks, but she didn't back down. "You're a cynical man, Dax Wakefield. Just because you don't believe in happily ever after doesn't mean it can't happen."

"True." He conceded the point with a nod. "And false. I readily admit to being cynical but happily ever after is a myth. Long-term relationships consist of two people who've agreed to put up with each other. No ridiculous lies about loving each other forever required."

"That's..." Apparently she couldn't come up with a word to describe it. So he helped her out.

"Reality?"

His mother had proven it by walking out on his father when Dax was seven. His father had never recovered from the hope she'd eventually come back. Poor sap.

"Sad," she corrected with a brittle smile. "You must be so lonely."

He blinked. "That's one I've never been called before. I could have five different dates lined up for tonight in about thirty seconds."

"Oh, you're in worse shape than I thought." With another slide of her legs that Dax couldn't quite ignore, she leaned toward him. "You need to meet the love of your life. Immediately. I can help you."

His own bark of laughter startled him. Because it wasn't funny. "Which part wasn't clear? The part where I said you were a phony or the part where I don't believe in love?"

"It was all very clear," she said quietly. "You're trying to prove my business, my life's work, is a sham. You can't, because I can find the darkest of hearts a match. Even yours. You want to prove something? Put your name in my computer."

Double ouch. He'd been bamboozled. And he'd never seen it coming.

Against all odds, he dredged up a healthy amount of respect for Elise Arundel.

Hell. He actually kind of liked her style.

* * *

Elise wiped her clammy hands on her skirt and prayed the pompous Mr. Wakefield didn't notice. This was not the scripted, safe interview she'd been promised or she never would have agreed to sit on this stage under all these burning hot lights, with what felt like a million pairs of eyes boring a hole through her.

Thinking on her feet was not her strong suit.

Neither was dealing with wealthy, spoiled, too-handsome, arrogant playboys who despised everything she believed in.

And she'd just invited him to test her skills. Had she accidentally inhaled paint thinner?

It hardly mattered. He'd never take her up on it. Guys like Dax didn't darken the door of a matchmaker. Shallow, unemotional relationships were a snap to find, especially for someone who clearly had a lot of practice enticing women into bed. And was likely an ace at keeping them there.

Dax stroked his jaw absently and contemplated her. "Are you offering to find me a match?"

"Not just a match," she corrected immediately and tore her gaze from the thumb running under his chiseled cheekbone. "True love. My gig is happily ever after."

Yes. It was, and she hadn't failed one single couple yet. She wasn't about to start today.

Matching hearts fulfilled her in so many ways. It almost made up for not finding her own match. But hope sprang eternal. If her mother's five marriages and dozens of affairs hadn't squeezed optimism and a belief in the power of love out of her, Dax Wakefield couldn't kill them either.

"So tell me about your own happily ever after. Is Mr. Arundel your one true love?"

"I'm single," she admitted readily. It was a common question from clients who wanted her credentials and the standard answer came easily now. "But it's not a commentary on my services. You don't decide against using a travel agent just because she hasn't been to the resort you're booking, right?"

"Right. But I would wonder why she became a travel agent if she doesn't ever get on a plane."

The crowd snickered and the muscles in her legs tensed. *Oh, spotlight how do I hate thee? Let me count the ways...*

She'd be happy to get on a plane if the right man came along. But clients were always right for someone else, not her, and well…she wasn't the best at walking up to interesting men in public and introducing herself. Friday nights with a chick flick always seemed safer than battling the doubts that she wasn't quite good enough, successful enough, or thin enough for dating.

She'd only agreed to this interview to promote her business. It was a necessary evil, and nothing other than EA International's success could entice her into making such a public spectacle.

"I always fly first class myself, Mr. Wakefield," she responded and if only her voice hadn't squeaked, the delivery would have been perfect. "As soon as you're ready to board, see me and I'll put you on the right plane in the right seat to the right destination.

"What do I have to do?" he asked. "Fill out a profile online?"

Was he actually considering it? She swallowed and the really bad feeling she'd tamped down earlier roared back into her chest.

Talk him out of it.

It was a stupid idea in the first place. But how else could she have responded? He was disparaging not only her profession but a company with her name on it.

"Online profiles don't work," she said. "In order

to find your soul mate, I have to know *you*. Personally."

Dax's eyelids drifted lower and he flashed a slumberous smile that absolutely should not have sent a zing through her stomach. "That sounds intriguing. Just how personal does this get, Ms. Arundel?"

Was he *flirting?* Well, she wasn't. This was cold, hard business. "Very. I ask a series of intensive questions. By the time I'm finished, I'll know you better than your own mother."

Something dark skittered through Dax's eyes but he covered it swiftly. "Tall order. But I don't kiss and tell, especially not to my mama. If I do this, what happens if I don't find true love? You'll be exposed as a fraud. Are you sure you're up for that?"

"I'm not worried," she lied. "The only thing I ask is that you take this seriously. No cheating. If you commit to the process and don't find true love, do your best to spread word far and wide that I'm not as good as I say I am."

But she *was* that good. She'd written the matching algorithm herself, pouring countless hours into the code until it was bulletproof. People often perplexed her, but a program either worked or it didn't, and she never gave up until she fixed the bug. Numbers were her refuge, her place of peace.

A well-written line of code didn't care how many chocolate bars she ate. Or how easily chocolate settled on her hips.

"That's quite a deal." His gaze narrowed. "But it's too easy. There's no way I can lose."

Because he believed she was pulling a fast one on her clients and that he'd never fall for it. "You're right. You don't lose either way. If you don't find love, you get to tear my business apart in whatever way makes sense to you. If you do find love, well…" She shrugged. "You'll be happy. And you'll owe me."

One brow quirked up and she refused to find it charming.

"Love isn't its own reward?"

He was toying with her. And he wasn't going to get away with it. "I run a business, Mr. Wakefield. Surely you can appreciate that I have expenses. Smoke and mirrors aren't free."

His rich laugh hit her crossways. Yeah, he had a nice laugh. It was the only nice anything he had that she'd admit to noticing. Dannie had certainly hit the mark when she described Dax Wakefield to

Elise as "yummy with an extra helping of cocky and a side of reptile."

"Careful, Ms. Arundel. You don't want to give away all your secrets on the morning news."

He shook his head, and his carefully coiffed hair bounced back into place. A guy as well put-together as Dax Wakefield hadn't even needed an hour with a makeup artist to be camera-ready. It was so unfair.

"I'm not giving anything away. Especially not my matchmaking abilities." Elise sat back in her chair. The farther away she was from Pretty Boy, the better. "So if you find true love, you'll agree to advertise my business. As a satisfied client."

His eyebrows shot up and the evidence of surprise gave her a little thrill that she wasn't at all ashamed to wallow in.

If this had been about anything other than EA International, the company she'd breathed life into for seven years, she'd have been at a loss for words, stumbling around looking for the exit.

But attacking her business made it personal. And for what? Because his friend had broken the guy code? Dax needed someone to blame for Leo's falling in love with Dannie, obviously, not that he'd admit it. Elise made a convenient scapegoat.

"You want me to advertise your services?" Incredulity laced his deep voice.

"If you find love, sure. I should get something out of this experiment, too. A satisfied client is the best reference." A satisfied client who'd previously denounced her skill set in public was worth more than a million dollars in advertising. "I'll even waive my fee if you do."

"Now you've got me curious. What's the going rate for true love these days?"

"Five hundred thousand dollars," she said flatly.

"That's outrageous." But he looked impressed nonetheless. About time she got his attention.

"I have dozens of clients who disagree. I guarantee my fees, too. If you don't find your soul mate, I refund your money. Well, not yours," she conceded with a nod. "You get to put me out of business."

That's when she realized her mistake. You could only find a soul mate for someone who had a soul. Dax Wakefield had obviously sold his a long time ago. This was never going to work. Her code would probably chew him up and spit him out.

She had to get off this stage before all these eyes and lights and camera lenses baked her like a pie.

Rubbing his hands together with something resembling glee, he winked. "A proposition I can't lose. I'm so on board with that, I'll even do you one better than a simple reference. Five hundred K buys a fifteen-second spot during the Super Bowl. If you pull a rabbit out of your hat and match me with my true love, I'll sing your praises right before halftime in a commercial starring *moi*."

"You will not." She let her gaze travel over his smooth, too-handsome face, searching for a clue to his real intentions.

Nothing but sincerity radiated back. "I will. Except I won't have to. You'll need a lot more than smoke and mirrors to win."

Win. As though this was a race.

"Why, because even if you fall in love, you'll pretend you haven't?"

A lethal edge sharpened his expression. "I gave you my word, Ms. Arundel. I might be a cynic, but I'm not a liar."

She'd offended him. His edges smoothed out so quickly, she would have thought she'd imagined it. But she knew what she'd seen. Dax Wakefield would not allow himself to win any other way than fair and square. And that decided it.

This…contest between them was about *her* as much as it was about EA International. As much about Dax's views on love and relationships ver-

sus hers. If she matched him with his soul mate—
not if, *when*—she'd prove once and for all that it
didn't matter what she looked like on the outside.
Matching people who wanted to fall in love was
easy. Finding a match for a self-professed cynic
would be a stellar achievement worthy of everyone's praise.

Her brain was her best asset and she'd dem-
onstrate it publicly. The short fat girl inside who
wanted her mother to love her regardless of Elise's
weight and height would finally be vanquished.

"Then it's a deal." Without hesitation, she slid
her hand into his and shook on it.

Something bold and electric passed between
them, but she refused to even glance at their joined
fingers. Unfortunately, whatever it was that felt
dangerous and the slightest bit thrilling came from
deep inside her and needed only Dax's dark gaze
to intensify it.

Oh, goodness. What had she just agreed to?

Two

The uncut footage was exceptional. Elise Arundel glowed on camera, just as Dax thought she would. The woman was stunning, animated. A real live wire. He peered at the monitor over the producer's shoulder and earned a withering glare from the man trying to do his job.

"Fine," Dax conceded with a nod to the producer. "Finish editing it and air the interview. It's solid."

Dallas's answer to a fairy godmother was going to wave her magic wand and give KDLS the highest ratings the news show had seen in two weeks. Maybe even in this whole fiscal year.

It was totally worth having to go through the motions of whatever ridiculous process Ms. Arundel cooked up. The failure to find him a soul mate would be so humiliating, Dax might not even go through with denouncing her company afterward.

But that all depended on how miserable Elise deliberately tried to make him. He had no doubt she'd give it her best shot.

Within fifteen minutes, the producer had the interview clip queued and ready. The station crew watched it unfold on the monitors. As Dax hammered the matchmaker, she held her own. The camera even captured the one instance she'd caught him off balance.

Okay, so it had happened twice, but no one other than Dax would notice—he was nothing if not a master at ensuring that everyone saw him precisely as he meant for them to.

Elise Arundel was something else, he'd give her that.

Shame those great legs were attached to such a misguided romantic, whom he should hate a lot more than he actually did. She'd refused to take any crap and the one-up she'd laid on him with the satisfied client bit…well, she'd done exactly what he'd have done in her shoes.

It had been kind of awesome. Or it would have

been if he'd escaped without agreeing to put his name in her computer.

Dax spent the rest of the day immersed in meetings with the station crew, hammering each department as easily as he had Elise. They had some preliminary numbers by lunch on the fairy godmother interview—and they were very good indeed—but one stellar day of ratings would not begin to make up for the last quarter.

As Dax slid into the driver's seat of his Audi, his phone beeped and he thumbed up the text message.

Jenna: You could have dates lined up with five different women? Since you're about to meet the love of your life...which is apparently not me...let's make it four. I never want to see you again.

Dax cursed. How bad was it that he'd forgotten Jenna would most assuredly watch the program? Maybe the worse crime was the fact that he'd forgotten entirely about the redhead he'd been dating for four—no, five—weeks. Or was it closer to six?

He cursed again. That relationship had stretched past its expiration date, but he'd been reluctant to give it up. Obviously Jenna had read more into it than she should have. They'd been having fun and he'd told her that was the extent of it. Regardless, she deserved better than to find out she had more of an investment than Dax from a TV program.

He was officially the worst sort of dog and should be shot.

Next time, he'd be clearer up front—Dax Wakefield subscribed to the Pleasure Principle. He liked his women fun, sexy and above all, unattached. Anything deeper than that was work, which he had enough of. Women should be about decadent indulgence. If it didn't feel good, why do it?

He drove home to the loft he'd bought in Deep Ellum before it was trendy and mentally scrolled through his contacts for just such a woman. Not one name jumped out. Probably every woman he'd ever spoken to had seen the clip. Didn't seem as if there were much point in getting shot down a few more times tonight.

But jeez, spending the night alone sucked.

Stomach growling, Dax dumped his messenger bag at the door and strode to the stainless-steel-and-black-granite kitchen to survey the contents of his cupboard.

While pasta boiled, he amused himself by recalling Elise's diabolical smile as she suggested Dax put his name in her computer. Sweet dreams were made of dark-haired, petite women.

He wasn't looking forward to being grilled about his favorite color and where he went to college so Ms. Arundel could pull a random woman's name out of her computer. But he was, oddly enough, looking forward to sparring with her some more.

The next morning, Dax opted to drive to his office downtown. He usually walked, both to get in the exercise and to avoid dealing with Dallas traffic, but Elise had scheduled their first session at the mutually agreed-upon time of 10:00 a.m.

By nine forty-seven, he'd participated in three conference calls, signed a contract for the purchase of a regional newspaper, read and replied to an inbox full of emails, and drunk two cups of coffee. Dax lived for Wakefield Media.

And now he'd have to sacrifice some of his day to the Fairy Godmother. Because he said he would.

Dax's mother was a coldhearted, untrustworthy woman, but in leaving, had taught him the importance of living up to your word. That was why he rarely promised anything.

EA International resided in a tasteful two-story office building in Uptown. The clean, low-key logo on the door spoke of elegance and sophistication, exactly the right tone to strike when your clients were high-powered executives and entrepreneurs.

The receptionist took his name. Dax proceeded to wait until finally she showed him to a room with two leather chairs and a low table strewn with picture books, one sporting a blue-and-gold fish on the cover and another, a waterfall.

Boring. Did Ms. Arundel hope to lull her clients into a semi-stupor while she let them cool their heels? Looked as though he was about to find out.

Elise clacked into the room, high heels against the hardwood floor announcing her presence. He glanced up slowly, taking in her heels, those well-built legs, her form-fitting scarlet skirt and jacket. Normally he liked taller women, but couldn't remember why just then. He kept going, thoroughly enjoying the trip to her face, which he'd forgotten was so arresting.

Her energy swept across him and prickled his skin, unnerving him for a moment. "You're late."

Her composed expression didn't waver. "You were late first."

Not that late. Ten minutes. Maybe. Regardless, she'd made him wait in this pseudo dentist's office on purpose. Score one for the matchmaker. "Trying to teach me a lesson?"

"I assumed you weren't going to show and took a call. I am running a business here." She settled into the second chair and her knee grazed his.

She didn't even seem to notice. His knee tingled but she simply crossed her legs and bounced one siren-red pump casually.

Just as casually, Dax tossed the fish book back on the table. "Busy day. The show does not go on without a lot of hands-on from yours truly."

But that didn't really excuse his tardiness. They were both business owners and he'd disrespected her. Unintentionally, but point taken.

"You committed to this. The profile session takes several hours. Put up or shut up."

Hours? He nearly groaned. How could it possibly take that long to find out he liked football, hated the Dallas Cowboys, drank beer but only dark and imported, and preferred the beach to the mountains?

Dax drew out his phone. "Give me your cell phone number." One of her eyebrows lowered and it was so cute, he laughed. "I'm not going to prank call you. If this is going to take hours, we'll have to split up the sessions. Then I can text you if I'm going to be late to the next one."

"Really?"

He shrugged, not certain why the derision in her tone raised his hackles. "Most women think it's considerate to let them know if you're held up. My apologies for assuming you fell into the category of females who appreciate a considerate man."

"Apology accepted. Now you know I'm in the category of woman who thinks texting is a cop-out. Try an actual phone call sometime." She smiled, baring her teeth, which softened the message not at all. "Better yet, just be punctual. Period."

She'd *accepted* his quasi-apology, as if he'd meant to really convey regret instead of sarcasm.

"Personal questions and punctuality?" He *tsk*ed to cover what he suspected might be another laugh trying to get out. When was the last time he'd been taken to task so expertly? Like never. "You drive a hard bargain, Ms. Arundel."

And she'd managed to evade giving out her digits. Slick. Not that he really wanted to call her. But still. It was kind of an amusing turnabout to be refused an attractive woman's phone number.

"You can call me Elise."

"Really?" It was petty repetition of her earlier succinct response. But in his shock, he'd let it slip.

"We're going to be working together. I'd like it if you were more comfortable with me. Hopefully it'll help you be more honest when answering the profile questions."

What was it about her and the truth? Did he look that much like a guy who skated the edge between black and white? "I told you I'm not a liar, whether I call you Elise, Ms. Arundel or sweetheart."

The hardness in her gaze melted, turning her irises a gooey shade of chocolate, and she sighed. "My turn to apologize. I can tell you don't want to be here and I'm a little touchy about it."

It was a rare woman who saw something other than what he meant for her to, and he did not want Elise to know anything about him, let alone against his will. Time for a little damage control.

"My turn to be confused. I do want to be here or I wouldn't have agreed to our deal. Why would you think otherwise?"

She evaluated his expression for a moment and tucked the straight fall of dark hair behind her ear, revealing a pale column of neck he had an un-explainable urge to explore. See if he could melt those hard eyes a little more. Unadulterated need coiled in his belly.

Down, boy.

Elise hated him. He didn't like her or anything she stood for. He was here to be matched with a woman who would be the next in a long line of ex-girlfriends and then declare EA International fraudulent. Because there was no way he'd lose this wager.

"Usually when someone is late, it's psychological," she said with a small tilt of her head, as if she'd found a puzzle to solve but couldn't quite get the right angle to view it.

"Are you trying to analyze me?"

She scowled. "It's not bargain-basement analysis. I have a degree in psychology."

"Yeah? Me, too."

They stared at each other for a moment, long enough for the intense spike in his abdomen to kick-start his perverse gene.

What was it about a smart woman that never failed to intrigue the hell out of him?

She broke eye contact and scribbled furiously in her notebook, color in her cheeks heightened.

She'd been affected by the heat, too.

He wanted to know more about Elise Arundel without divulging anything about himself that wasn't surface-level inanity.

"The information about my major was a freebie," he said. "Anything else personal you want to know is going to cost you."

If they were talking about Elise—and didn't every woman on the planet prefer to talk about herself?—Dax wouldn't inadvertently reveal privileged information. That curtain was closed, and no one got to see backstage.

Elise was almost afraid to ask. "Cost me what?"

When Dax's smoke-colored eyes zeroed in on her, she was positive she should be both afraid *and* sorry. His irises weren't the black smoke of an angry forest fire, but the wispy gray of a late November hearth fire that had just begun to blaze. The kind of fire that promised many delicious, warm things to come. And could easily burn down the entire block if left unchecked.

"It'll cost you a response in kind. Whatever you ask me, you have to answer, too."

"That's not how this works. I'm not trying to match myself."

Though she'd been in the system for seven years.

She'd entered her profile first, building the code around the questions and answers. On the off chance a match came through, well, there was nothing wrong with finding her soul mate with her own process, was there?

"Come on. Be a sport. It'll help me be more comfortable with baring my soul to you."

She shook her head hard enough to flip the ends of her hair into her mouth. "The questions are not all that soul-baring."

Scrambling wasn't her forte any more than thinking on her feet, because that was a total misrepresentation. The questions were designed to strip away surface-level BS and find the real person underneath. If that wasn't soul-baring, she didn't know what was. How else could the algorithm find a perfect match? The devil was in the details, and she had a feeling Dax's details could upstage Satan himself.

"Let's find out," he said easily. "What's the first one?"

"Name," she croaked.

"Daxton Ryan Wakefield. Daxton is my grandmother's maiden name. Ryan is my father's name." He shuddered in mock terror. "I feel exposed sharing my history with a virtual stranger. Help a guy out. Your turn."

This was so not a good idea. But he'd threatened her business, her livelihood. To prove her skills, his profile had to be right. Otherwise, he might be matched with an almost–soul mate or worse, someone completely incompatible. Dax wasn't a typical paying client, and she couldn't treat him like one. What was the harm in throwing him one bone? It wasn't as if she had to answer all of the questions, just enough to get him talking.

"Shannon Elise Arundel."

How in the world had that slipped out? She hadn't told anyone that her real first name was Shannon in years. Her shudder of terror wasn't faked.

Shannon, put down that cake. Shannon, have you weighed yourself today? Shannon, you might be vertically challenged but you don't have to be horizontally challenged too.

The words were always delivered with the disapproving frown her mother saved for occasions of great disappointment. Frowning caused wrinkles and Brenna Burke hated wrinkles more than photographers.

Dax circled his finger in a get-on-with-the-rest motion. "No comment about how your father was Irish and wanted to make sure you had a bit of the old country in your name?"

"Nope. My name is very boring."

Her mother was the Irish one, with milky skin and glowing red hair that graced magazine covers and runways for twenty years. Brenna Burke, one of the world's original supermodels, had given birth to a short Black Irish daughter prone to gaining weight by simply looking at cookies. It was a sin of the highest order in Brenna's mind that Elise had a brain instead of beauty.

Dax quirked his mouth in feigned disappointment. "That's okay. We can't all have interesting stories attached to our names. Where did you grow up?"

"This is not a date." The eye roll happened involuntarily, but the exasperation in her voice was deliberate. "I'm asking the questions."

"It's kind of like a date," he mused brightly as if the thought fascinated him. "Getting to know each other. Awkward silences. Both of us dressed just a little bit more carefully than normal."

She glanced down at her BCBG suit, which she'd snipped the tags from that morning. Because red made her feel strong and fierce, and a session with Dax called for both. So what? "This is how I dress every day."

Now she felt self-conscious. Did the suit and five-inch stilettos seem as though she was trying too hard?

"Then I'm really looking forward to seeing what you look like tomorrow." He waggled his brows.

"Let's move on," she said before Dax drove her insane. "This is not a date, nor is it kind of like a date, and I'm getting to know you, not the other way around. So I can find you a match."

"Too bad. A date is the best place to see me in action." When she snorted, he inclined his head with a mischievous smile. "That's not what I meant, but since you started it, my favorite part of dates is anticipating the first kiss. What's yours?"

She lifted her gaze from his parted lips and blinked at the rising heat in his expression. The man had no shame. Flirting with his matchmaker, whose business he was also trying to destroy.

"Jedi mind tricks only work on the weak-minded. Tell me more about what you like about dating. It's a great place to start."

He grinned and winked. "Deflection only works on those who graduated at the bottom of their class. But I'll let it pass this time. I like long walks on the beach, hot tubs and dinner for two on the terrace."

Clearly this was slated to be the battle of who had the better psychology degree. Fine. *You want to play, let's play.*

"Why don't you try again, but this time without the *Love Connection* sound bite? I didn't ask what you liked to *do* on dates. I asked what you like about *dating*."

"I like sex," he said flatly. "In order to get that, dating is a tiresome requirement. Is that what you're looking for?"

"Not really. Plus it's not true." His irises flashed from hearth-fire smoke to forest-fire smoke instantly and she backpedaled. "I don't mean you're lying. Get a grip. I mean, you don't have to date someone to have sex. Lots of women would gladly line up for a roll in the sheets with a successful, sophisticated man."

Who had a face too beautiful to be real, the physique of an elite athlete and eyelashes her mother would kill for. Not that she'd noticed.

"Would you?"

"I don't do one-night stands."

She frowned. When was the last time she'd even been on a date? Oh, yeah, six months ago—Kory, with a *K*. She should have known that one wouldn't work out the instant he'd introduced himself as such.

"There you go. A woman who would isn't worth my time."

Her head snapped back. Was that a compliment? More flirting? The truth?

"So you aren't just looking for sex. You want to put some effort into a relationship. Have drinks, spend some time together. And you want to know things about the women you date, their history, their likes and dislikes. Why?"

He contemplated her as he sat back in his chair, thumb to his jaw, a habit she'd noticed he fell into when she made the wheels in his convoluted head turn. Good.

"You're much more talented than I imagined," he allowed with a jerk of his chin. "I'm so impressed, I'm going to tell you why. It's so I can buy her something she'd genuinely appreciate and give it to her on our next date."

So the woman in question would sleep with him, no doubt. And it probably never failed. "Another example of a considerate man?"

"Sure. Women like to be treated well. I like women. Ergo, it's no chore to do my best to make them happy."

There had to be something wrong with that, but she couldn't find the fault to save her life. Plus, the glow from his compliment still burned brightly. "If only all men subscribed to that theory. What do you find attractive in a woman?"

"Brains," he said instantly and she didn't even bother to write that down.

"You can't tell if a woman has brains from across the room," she responded drily. "If you walk into a bar, who catches your eye?"

"I don't meet women in bars, and last time I walked into one, I got four stitches right here." He tapped his left eyebrow, which was bisected by a faint line, and his chagrined smile was so infectious, she couldn't help but laugh.

"Okay, you win that round. But I have to note something. Redhead, blonde? Voluptuous, athletic?"

"Would you believe it if I said I have no preference? Or at least that used to be true." He swept her with a sizzling once-over that curled her toes involuntarily. "I might be reconsidering."

"The more you try to unsettle me, the less it works," she advised him and cursed the catch in her throat that told him her actual state far better than her words. This was ridiculous and getting them nowhere. "You promised to take this seriously and all I know about you so far is that distraction and verbal sleight of hand are your standard operating procedure. What are you hiding?"

The flicker of astonishment darting through his

expression vanished when a knock sounded on the door. Dang it. She'd hardly begun to dig into the good stuff.

Elise's assistant, Angie, stuck her head in and said, "Your next appointment is here."

Both she and Dax shot startled glances at their watches. When he hadn't shown, she'd scheduled another appointment. How had the minutes vanished so quickly?

He stood immediately. "I'm late for a meeting."

What did it say that they'd both lost track of the hour? She nodded. "Tomorrow, then. Same time, same bat channel?"

He grinned. "You've got yourself a date, Ms. Arundel."

Three

Dax whistled a nameless tune as he pulled open the door to EA International. Deliberately late, and not at all sorry.

Today, he was in charge, and Elise would not get the drop on him again. He'd give her enough information to make it seem that he was going along willingly, simultaneously dragging out their interaction a little longer. Long enough to figure out what about Elise got under his skin, anyway. Then he was done here.

"Morning, Angie." Dax smiled at the receptionist and handed her the vase of stargazer lilies he'd brought. "For you. Is Ms. Arundel's calendar free?"

Angie moistened her lips and smiled in return.

"Cleared, just as you requested yesterday. Thanks for the flowers. They're beautiful."

"I'll show myself to Ms. Arundel's office." He winked. "Don't tell her I'm coming. It's a surprise."

When Dax blew through the door of Elise's office, the location of which he'd noted yesterday on his way out, the look on her face was more wary disbelief than surprise.

"Look what the cat dragged in," was all she said and ignored him in favor of typing on her laptop. The clacking was too rhythmic to produce actual comprehensible sentences.

Faking it. For him. Warmed his heart.

"I'm taking you to lunch," he informed her. "Get your handbag and shut that thing down."

That earned her attention. She pierced him with that laser-sharp gaze he suspected had the power to drill right through his skull and read his mind like a book. "Are you this egotistical with all women? I'm shocked you ever get a second date."

"Yet I do. Have lunch with me and you'll find out why." He quirked a brow at her and pulled out the big guns. "Unless you're afraid."

She didn't scowl, didn't immediately negate the statement. Instead, she smiled and clicked the laptop closed. "Can't stand being under the spotlight, can you? If you don't like the setting I use to walk through the profile questions, just tell me."

A spontaneous and unexpected laugh shot from his mouth. Why was it such a surprise that she was on to him?

He held up both hands. "I surrender. You're right. That little room with the fish book is like being in therapy. Restaurants are more relaxed."

Elise opened a desk drawer and withdrew a brown leather bag. "Since my schedule is mysteriously clear, lunch it is. On one condition." She cocked her head, sending her dark hair swinging against her chin. "Don't evade, change the subject or try to outsmart me. Answer the questions so we can be done."

"Aww. You're not enjoying this?" He was. It was the most fun he'd had with a woman he wasn't dating in his life.

"You're quite honestly the most difficult, disturbing, contrary client I've ever dealt with." She swept passed him in a cloud of unidentifiable perfume that hit him in the solar plexus, and then she shot back over her shoulder, "Which means you're paying. But I'm driving."

He grinned and followed her to the parking lot, then slid into the passenger seat of the sleek Corvette she motioned to. He would have opened her door, but she beat him to it.

New car smell wrapped around him. "Nice ride. I pegged you for more of a Toyota girl."

She shrugged. "Even fairy godmothers like to arrive at the ball in style."

"I'm not threatened by a woman driving, by the way." He crossed his arms so he didn't accidentally brush shoulders with Elise. The seats were really close together. Perfect for lovers. Not so good for business associates. "Just in case you were worried."

Elise selected an out-of-the-way bistro-type place without asking him and told the hostess they'd prefer to sit outside, also without his input. The wrought iron chairs and tables on the terrace added French charm and the wine list was passable, so he didn't mind. But two could play that game, so he ordered a bottle of Chianti and nodded to the waiter to pour Elise a glass whether she wanted one or not.

"To loosen you up?" she asked pertly and picked up her glass to sniff the bloodred wine with appreciation.

"Nah. To loosen you up." He dinged their rims together and watched her drink. Elise liked red wine. He filed that tidbit away. "I didn't actually agree to your condition, you know."

"I noticed. I'm banking on the fact that you're a busy man and can't continually take time away from work to finish something you don't want to be doing in the first place. So don't disappoint me. What's the difference between love, romance and sex?"

Dax choked on the wine he'd just swallowed and spent his time recovering. "Give a guy a warning before you lay that kind of question on him."

"Warning. Question imminent. Warning. Question imminent," she intoned in such a perfect robot voice, he sputtered over a second sip, laughing this time.

For an uptight matchmaker, she had an offbeat sense of humor. He liked it. More than he should. It was starting to affect his focus and the more Elise charmed him, the less he remembered why it was important to punish her for Leo's defection.

"Let's see," he said brusquely. "Fiction, Sade and yes, please."

"Excuse me?"

"The answer to your question. Love equals fiction, Sade is romantic music and critical to set the mood, and I would assume 'yes, please' is self-explanatory in relation to sex."

"That's not precisely what I was looking for."

"Then tell me what you would say. So I have an example to go by."

"You never give up, do you?"

"Took you long enough to figure that out. So?" he prompted with raised eyebrows.

She sighed. "They're intertwined so closely you can't remove one without destroying the value of the other two."

"That's a loaded statement. Tell me more before I proceed to tear it apart." He propped his chin on his hand and ignored the halibut a waiter placed in front of him, which he scarcely recalled ordering.

Her lips mushed together in apparent indecision. Or frustration. Hard to tell with her.

"You can have sex without being in love or putting on romantic music. But it's so much better with both. Without love and romance, sex is meaningless and empty."

As she warmed to the topic, her expression softened and that, plus the provocative subject matter, plus the warm breeze playing with her hair, plus…whatever it was about her that drew him all swirled together and spread like a sip of very old, very rare cognac in his chest. "Go on."

"On the flip side, you can certainly make a romantic gesture toward someone you're in love with and not end up in bed. But the fact that you've been intimate magnifies it. Makes it more romantic. See what I mean?"

"Philosophy." He nodded sagely and wondered if the thing going on inside might be a heart attack. "I see. You want to understand how I feel about the three, not give you examples. Rookie mistake. Won't happen again."

"Ha. You did it on purpose so you could probe me."

That was so close to the truth, the back of his neck heated. Next his ears would turn red and no woman got to have that strong of an effect on him. "Yeah, well, guess what? I like the spotlight. When you accused me of that earlier, it was nothing but a classic case of projection. You don't like the spotlight so you assumed that was the reason I didn't want to sit under yours."

She didn't so much as flinch. "Then what is the reason you went to such great lengths to get me out of the office?"

The shrewd glint in the depths of those chocolaty irises tipped him off that he hadn't been as slick with the schedule-clearing as he believed. Odds were, she'd also figured out that she'd hit a couple of nerves yesterday and lunch was designed to prevent that from happening again.

"That's your turf." He waved at the crowd of tables, people and ambiance. "This is mine."

"And I'm on it, with nary a peep. Cut me some slack. Tell me what your ideal mate brings to the relationship."

"A lack of interest in what's behind the curtain," he said instantly as if the answer had been there all along. Though he'd never so much as thought about the question, not once, and certainly wouldn't have told her if she hadn't made the excellent point about the turf change.

But lack of interest wasn't quite right. It was more the ability to turn a blind eye. Someone who saw through the curtain and didn't care that backstage resembled post-tornado wreckage.

Was that why he broke up with women after the standard four weeks—none thus far had that X-ray-vision-slash-blind-eye quality?

"Good." Elise scribbled in her ever-present notebook. "Now tell me what you bring to her."

When she'd called the questions intensive, she wasn't kidding. "What, presents aren't enough?"

"Don't be flip. Unless you want me to assume you bring nothing to a relationship and that's why you shy away from them." A light dawned in her eyes. "Oh. That's it, isn't it? You don't think you have anything to offer."

"Wait a minute. That's not what I said." This conversation had veered way too far off the rails for comfort.

He'd agreed to this ridiculous idea of being matched only because he never thought it would work. Instead, Elise challenged his deep-seated beliefs at every turn with a series of below-the-belt hits. That was not supposed to happen.

"Then say what you mean," she suggested quietly. "For once. If you found that woman, the one who didn't care what was behind your curtain, what do you have to offer her in return?"

"I don't know." It was the most honest answer he could give. And the most unsettling.

He shoveled food in his mouth in case she asked a follow-up question.

What *did* he have to offer in a relationship? He'd never considered it important to examine, largely because he never intended to have a relationship. But he felt deficient all at once.

"Fair enough. I get that these questions are designed to help people who are looking for love. You're not. So we'll move on to the lightning round." Her sunny tone said she knew she was letting him off the hook and it was okay.

Oddly grateful, he nodded and relaxed. "I rule at lightning rounds."

"We'll see, Mr. Wakefield. Glass half-full, or half-empty?"

"Technically, it's always full of both air and water." Her laugh rumbled through him and he breathed a little easier. Things were clicking along at a much safer level now, and eating held more appeal.

"That's a good one. Apple or banana?"

"What is that, a Freudian question? Apple, of course."

"Actually, apples have biblical connotations. I might interpret it as you can't stay away from the tree of knowledge," she said with a smirk. "What relieves stress?"

"Sex."

She rolled her eyes. "I probably didn't need to ask that one. Do you believe in karma?"

These were easy, surface-level questions. She should have started with them. "No way. Lots of people never get what's coming to them."

"That is *so* true." She chuckled with appreciation and shook her head.

"Don't freak out but I do believe you're enjoying this after all."

Her smile slipped but she didn't look away. This might not be a date, but he couldn't deny that lunch with Elise was the most interesting experience he'd had with a woman, period. Even ones he was dating.

The longer this went on, the harder it was going to be to denounce her publicly. She was good—much better than he'd prepared for—and to criticize her abilities would likely reflect just as poorly on him as it did her.

Worse, he was afraid he'd started to like her. He should probably do something about that before she got too far under his skin.

By one o'clock, Elise's side hurt from laughing. Wine at lunch should be banned. Or required. She couldn't decide which.

"I have to get back to the office," she said reluctantly.

Reluctantly? She had a ton of things to do. And this was lunch with Dax. Whom she hated...or rather didn't like very much. Actually, he was pretty funny and maybe a little charming. Of course he was—he had lots of practice wooing women.

Dax made a face. "Yeah. Duty calls."

He stood and gallantly took her hand, while simultaneously pulling her chair away. It was amazingly well-coordinated. Probably because he'd done it a million times.

They strolled to the car and she pretended that she didn't notice how slowly, and she didn't immediately fish her keys from her bag. Dax put his palm on the driver's-side door, leaning against it casually, so she couldn't have opened it anyway. Deliberately on his part, she was sure.

She should call him on it.

"Tomorrow, then?" he asked.

Elise shook her head. "I'm out of the office tomorrow. I have a thing with my mother."

Brenna had an appointment with a plastic surgeon in Dallas because the ones in L.A. stopped living up to her expectations. Apparently she couldn't find one who could make her look thirty again.

"All day?" Dax seemed disappointed. "You can't squeeze in an hour for me?"

No way was he disappointed. She shook her head. The wine was affecting her more than she'd thought.

"I have to pick her up from the airport and then take her to the doctor." Oh, that might have been too much information. "I need to ask for your discretion. She wouldn't like it if she knew I was talking to others about her private affairs."

"Because your mother is famous or something?"

Elise heaved a sigh. "I assumed you checked up on me and therefore already knew I was Brenna Burke's daughter. I should have kept my mouth shut."

Stupid wine.

"Brenna Burke is your mother?" Dax whistled. "I had a poster of her above my bed when I was a teenager. The one where she wore the bikini made of leaves. Good times."

"Thanks, I needed the image in my head of you fantasizing about my mother." That's precisely why she never mentioned Brenna. Not only because of the ick factor, but also because no one ever whistled over Elise. It was demoralizing. "You know she was thirty-five in that photo, right?"

Elise called it her mother's I'm-not-old stage, when the hot runway models were closer to her nine-year-old daughter's age than Brenna's, and the offers of work had all but dried up.

I should have waited to have kids, Brenna had told her. *Mistake Number One talked me into it. Being pregnant and off the circuit ruined me.*

Bitter, aging supermodels took out their frustration on those around them, including Elise's father, dubbed Mistake Number One when he grew tired of Brenna's attitude and left. Adult Elise knew all this from her psychology classes. Still hurt, even years later.

"So?" Dax sighed lustily. "I didn't care. She was smoking hot."

"Yeah. So I've been told." She feigned sudden interest in her manicure, unable to take the appreciation for her mother in Dax's expression.

"Elise." His voice held a note of...warmth. Compassion.

Somehow, he'd steered her around, spine against the car, and then he was right there, sandwiching her between his masculine presence and the Vette.

He tipped her head up with a fist and locked those smoky irises on hers and she couldn't breathe. "Tastes change. I like to think I've evolved since

I was fourteen. Older women aren't so appealing anymore."

She shrugged. "Whatever. It hardly matters."

"It does." The screeches and hums of the parking lot and chatter of other diners faded away as he cocked his head and focused on her. "I hurt your feelings. I'm sorry."

How in the world had he figured that out? Somehow, that fact alone made it easy to admit the truth. She probably couldn't have hidden it anyway. "It's hard to have a mother known for her looks when you're so average, you know?"

He shifted closer, though she would have sworn there wasn't much space between them in the first place.

"You're the least average woman I've ever met, and you know what else? Beauty fades. That's why it's important to use what's up here." He circled an index finger around her temple, oh so slowly, and the electrified feel of his touch on her skin spread through her entire body.

"That's my line," she murmured. "I went to college and started my own business because I never wanted a life where my looks mattered."

After watching her mother crash and burn with

Mistake Number Two and then Three without finding the happiness she seemed to want so desperately, Elise learned early on that a relationship built on physical attraction didn't work. It also taught her that outward appearance hardly factored in matters of the heart.

Compatibility and striving to find someone who made you better were the keys to a relationship. She'd built EA International on those principles, and it hadn't failed yet.

Dax was so close; she inhaled his exotic scent on her next breath. It screamed *male—and how*.

"Me, too. Unlike your mother, I never wanted to make a career out of modeling." When her eyebrows shot up, he chuckled. "Figured you checked up on me and knew that Calvin Klein put me through college. Guess you'll be looking me up when you get home."

A lit stick of dynamite between her and the laptop couldn't stop that from happening. "My mother put me through college. Reluctantly, but I insisted."

Funny how they'd both paid for college with modeling dollars and then took similar paths to chart their own destinies. She never would have guessed they had anything in common, let alone such important guiding experiences.

Dax's gaze drifted lower and focused on her mouth. Because he was thinking about kissing her. She could read it all over his expression.

Emergency. This wasn't a date. She'd led him on somehow. They didn't like each other, and worse, he shied away from everything she desired—love, marriage, a soul mate. She was supposed to be matching him with one of her clients.

First and foremost, she'd given him permission to *ruin her business* if he didn't find the love of his life. And she was compromising the entire thing.

All of it swirled into a big black burst of panic. Had she lost her mind?

Ducking clumsily out of his semi-embrace, she smiled brightly. "So I'll call you to schedule the next session. Ready to go?"

His expression shuttered and he nodded. "Sure. I'll leave you my card with my number."

In awkward silence, they rode back to EA International where Dax's car was parked.

Despite knowing he thought happily ever after was a myth, despite knowing he faked interest in her as a method of distraction, despite knowing he stood to lose $500,000 and pretended to misunderstand her questions or refused to answer them strictly to prevent it—despite all that, she'd wanted him to kiss her.

Dax Wakefield was better at seducing a woman than she'd credited.

When Elise got to her office, she locked the door and sank into the chair. Her head fell forward into her cupped palms, too wined-and-Daxed to stay upright any longer. If he flipped her out this much without laying those gorgeously defined lips on hers, how much worse would it be if he'd actually done it?

She couldn't take another session with him.

Match him now.

She had enough information. Dax might have thought he was being sneaky by probing her for answers to the questions in kind but he'd revealed more about himself in the getting there than he likely realized.

While the match program booted up, Elise stuck a stick of gum in her mouth in hopes it would stave off the intense desire for chocolate. She always craved chocolate, but it was worse when she was under stress.

Maybe she should take a page from Dax and relieve her stress with sex.

But not with him. No sir.

Almost of their own accord, her fingers keyed his name into the browser. Provocative photos spilled onto the screen of a younger Dax with washboard abs and formfitting briefs scarcely covering the good parts. Her mouth went dry. The man was a former underwear model with a psychology degree, a wicked sense of humor and a multibillion-dollar media empire.

Who in the world did she have in her system to match *that?*

Usually she had a pretty good idea who the match would be ahead of time. One of the benefits of administering the profile sessions herself—she knew her clients very well.

A slice of fear ripped through her. What if the program couldn't find a match? It happened occasionally. The algorithms were so precise that sometimes clients had to wait a few months, until she entered new clients.

Dax would never accept that excuse. He'd call foul and claim victory right then and there. Either he'd crow about proving Elise a sham or worse, claim she'd withheld the name on purpose to avoid the fallout when the match wasn't the love of his life.

Newly determined, she shut down the almost-naked pictures of Dax and flipped to the profile screen. She flew through the personal information section and consulted her notes before starting on the personality questions.

That went easily, too. In fact, she didn't even have to glance at the scribbled words in her notebook.

Do you want to be in love? She typed yes. He did, he just hadn't found the right person yet, or he wouldn't have agreed to be matched. Plus, she'd watched his face when he described a woman who didn't care about whatever he hid behind his curtain. That man wanted to connect really, really badly with someone who got him.

How do you sabotage relationships? She snorted and typed "by only dating women he has no chance of falling in love with."

When she reached the last question, she breathed a sigh of relief. Not so bad. Thank goodness she wouldn't have to see him again. A quick phone call to set up his first meet with the match and she'd be done with Dax Wakefield.

She hit Save and ran the match algorithm. Results came back instantly. Fantastic. She might even treat herself to half a carton of Chunky Monkey as a reward. She clicked on the pop-up link and Dax's match was…*Elise Arundel*.

No! She blinked, but the letters didn't change.

That was so wrong, she couldn't even put words together to say how wrong.

She ran the compiler again. *Elise Arundel*.

Stomach cramping with dread, she vised her temples. That's what she got for not asking him all the questions. For letting her professional ethics slide away in the wake of the whirlwind named Dax.

He'd think she did it on purpose—because she'd started to fall for his slick charm. If she actually told him she was his match, he'd smirk with that knowing glint in his eyes and…

She'd skewed the results. That had to be it. Talk about your Freudian slipups—she'd been thinking about the almost-kiss and the almost-naked pictures and his laugh and thus answered the questions incorrectly.

Besides, the short, fat girl inside could never be enough to change Dax Wakefield's mind about love. She had to match him with someone else.

Her fingers shook and she could hardly type, but those answers had to change. He didn't want to be in love. Total projection on her part to say that he did, exactly as he'd accused her of earlier. She fixed that one, then the next one and eventually worked her way back through the profile

There. She clicked Run and shut her eyes.

This time, the pop-up opened to reveal...Candace Waters.

Perfect. Candy was a gorgeous blonde with a high-school education. Dax would love running intellectual circles around her and Candy liked football. They'd get along famously.

No one ever had to know Elise had nearly screwed up.

Four

When an unrecognized number flashed on Dax's phone, he almost didn't answer it.

Instead of working, as he should be, he'd been watching his phone, hoping Elise might call today.

He couldn't get that moment against the car out of his head, that brief flicker in her gaze that said she didn't hate him anymore and better yet, didn't see him as a match to be pawned off on some other female. Before he'd had time to explore what she did feel, she'd bolted, leaving him to wonder if he'd imagined it.

He should call her already. It was only a conversation to schedule the next session, which would likely be the last. What was the big deal about calling? It wasn't as if she'd answer the main line at EA International anyway. He could schedule the appointment through Angie and go on with his day.

The quicker they finished the sessions, the closer Elise would be to be finding him a match, at which point he'd prove beyond a shadow of a doubt that Elise's matchmaking service fronted as a school for gold diggers. Then, the cold place inside that had developed during the rift with Leo could be warmed nicely by the flames of EA International roasting on the morning news.

A prospect that held less and less appeal the more time he spent with Elise.

The dilemma ate at him, and if he didn't see her again, he didn't have to think about it. That's why he didn't call.

But Dax answered his phone, mentally preparing to spiel off a contract's status or sales figures—pending the caller's identification. "Wakefield."

"It's Elise Arundel." The smooth syllables hit him in all the right places. "Do you have a few minutes?"

He should have called her. Elise had a sexy phone voice.

Grinning like a loon for who knew what reason, Dax settled back in his chair and put his feet out. "Depends on what for. If it's lightning round two, yes."

Elise's chuckle was a little on the nervous side. "I'm afraid that's not the reason for my call. Actually, I have good news on that front. More sessions aren't required after all. I've got your match."

Oh, wow. This thing had just become nauseatingly real.

"Already? That is good news," Dax said heartily. It *was* good news. The best. He didn't have to see Elise again, exactly as he wanted.

And a little voice inside was singing, *Liar, liar, pants on fire.*

"So," Elise chimed in quickly, "I'm calling to set up your first meet with your match, Candace. She prefers to be called Candy, though."

"Candy." That was something you ate, not someone you dated, and sounded suspiciously like a name for a coed. "She's legal, right?"

"You mean is she over the age of eighteen?" Elise's withering tone put the grin back on his face. "What kind of matchmaker do you take me for? She's twenty-eight and works as a paralegal for Browne and Morgan."

"Just checking. What's the drill? I'm supposed to call her and set up a date or something?"

"That's up to you. I've emailed her picture to you, and I've sent yours to her. If you're both agreeable to meeting, I'd be happy to coordinate or you can go it alone from here."

Curiosity got the best of him and he shouldered the phone to his ear so he could click through his email. There it was—"Sender: Elise Arundel, Subject: Candace Waters." He opened it and a picture of Candy popped onto the screen.

Holy hell. She was *gorgeous*. Like men-falling-over-themselves-to-get-her-a-drink gorgeous. Not at all what he was expecting. "Is she one of your makeover success stories?"

If so, Elise might have a bit more magic in her wand than he'd credited.

"Not everyone is in need of a makeover. Candy came to me as is."

Nice. Not a gold digger then. He took a closer look. She was blonde-with-a-capital-B, wearing a wicked smile that promised she had the moves to back it up. He would have noticed her across the room in a heartbeat.

For the first time, he got an inkling that this whole deal might be legitimate. "She'll do."

Then he returned to planet earth. There was a much greater chance that Candy had something really wrong with her if she'd resorted to a match-maker to find a date.

"I had a feeling you'd like her," Elise said wryly. "She's perfect for you."

Because something was really wrong with him too?

Elise was obviously running around wielding her psychology degree like a blunt instrument. She'd probably come up with all kinds of bogus analyses about his inability to commit and his mama issues—bogus because he didn't have a problem committing as long as the thing had Wakefield Media stamped on it. Females were a different story. He'd die before letting a woman down the way his mother had let down his father, and he'd never met someone worth making that kind of promise to.

No doubt Elise had warned Candy about what she'd gotten herself into. Maybe she'd given Candy hints about how to get under his skin. Elise certainly had figured out how to do that well enough. And of course Elise had a vested interest in making sure Candy made him happy. This woman he'd been matched with might even be a plant. Some actress Elise had paid to get him to fall in love with her.

That...*schemer.*

Thank God he never had to see Elise again. A paralegal sounded like a blessed reprieve from razor-sharp matchmakers with great legs.

"I'll call her. Then I expect you'll want a full report afterward, right?"

The line went dead silent.

"Still there, Elise?"

"Not a *full* report."

"About whether she's my soul mate. Get your mind out of the gutter."

For some reason, that made Elise laugh and muscles he hadn't realized were tense relaxed.

"Yeah, I do want that report. I guess we never really laid down the ground rules of how this deal was going to go. Do we need an unbiased third party to verify the results?"

A judge? Suddenly, he felt like a bug pinned to cork. "The fewer people involved in this, the better. I'll call you afterward and we'll go from there. How's that?"

"Uncomplicated. I can get on board with that. Have a good time with Candy. Talk to you later."

The line went dead for the second time and Dax

immediately saved Elise's number to his contacts. It gave him a dark little kick to have the matchmaker's phone number when she'd been so adamantly against giving it to him.

Then he dialed Candy's number, which Elise had included with the picture. His perverse gene wanted to find out if Candy was on the up-and-up. If Elise had hired someone to date him, he'd cry foul so fast it would make her head spin. And he'd never admit it was exactly what he'd have done.

Dax handed the valet his Audi's key fob and strolled into the wine bar Candy had selected for their first meet. She wasn't difficult to find—every eye in the room was on the sultry blonde perched on a bar stool.

Then every eye in the room turned to fixate on him as he moved forward to buss Candy on the cheek. "Hi. Nice place."

They'd conversed on the phone a couple of times. She had a pleasant voice and seemed sane, so here they were.

She peered up at him out of china doll–blue eyes that were a little less electric in person than they'd been on his laptop screen. No big deal. Her sensual vibe definitely worked for his Pleasure Principle—she'd feel good, all right, and better the second time.

"You look exactly like your picture," she said, her voice a touch breathier than it had been on the phone. "I thought you'd swiped it from a magazine and you'd turn out to be average-looking. I'm glad I was wrong."

Dax knew what reflected back at him in the mirror; he wasn't blind, and time had been kind to his features. It was stupid to be disappointed that she'd commented on his looks first. But why did his cheekbones have to be the first thing women noticed about him?

Most women. He could have been wearing a paper bag over his head for all the notice Elise had taken of his outward appearance. One of the first things she'd said to him was that he was lonely.

And as Candy blinked at him with a hint of coquettishness, he experienced an odd sense of what Elise meant. Until a woman ripped that curtain back and saw the man underneath the skin, it was all just going through the motions. And Dax dated women incapable of penetrating his cynical hide.

How had he just realized that?

And how *dare* Elise make him question his dating philosophy? If she was so smart, why hadn't she figured out he was dating the wrong women?

Besides, he wasn't. The women he dated were fine. Ms. Arundel was *not* ruining this date with her psychobabble.

He slid into the vacant bar stool next to Candy, swiveled it toward her and gave her his best, most practiced smile. It always knocked 'em dead. "You look like your picture, too. Have you ever modeled?"

Dax signaled to the bartender to bring a wine menu and tapped the Chilean red without glancing at it for more than a moment. Ordering wine was a necessary skill and he'd had plenty of opportunity to develop it. Regardless of whether this woman was his soul mate or Elise's accomplice, she'd appreciate his taste.

She nodded. "Since I was fourteen. Regional print mostly, department stores, catalogs, that kind of thing. Celebrities took over cosmetics so I never had a chance there, but eventually all the offers stopped. My mom made me get a job with benefits when I turned twenty-five."

It had been a throwaway question, one you asked a woman as a compliment, but she'd taken it seriously, reeking of sincerity as she'd talked. "So you're a paralegal now?"

She wrinkled her nose and laughed. The combination was cute. Not perky cheerleader let-me-make-you-a-cupcake cute. Actually, it wasn't so cute at all, in retrospect.

"Yes, I research legal briefs all day," she said. "It's not what I imagined myself doing, but it was so hard to find a job. If a woman interviewed me, I got shown the door immediately. Men were worse. You can bet they made it clear the job was mine if I agreed to 'after hours' work."

Candy shuddered delicately and Dax had no problem interpreting what "after hours" meant. "Discrimination at its finest."

"Most people think it's a nice problem to have. It's not. I get so beat down by people who judge me by my looks." Crossing her legs casually, Candy leaned forward and rested an elbow on the bar to casually dangle her hand an inch above Dax's knee. "That's why I signed up with EA International. I can't meet men the traditional way."

Her body language screamed *I'm into you*. The benefit of understanding human psychology—people rarely surprised him. And Candy was legit. He'd stake his life on it.

"I get that. Who wants to meet someone in a crowded bar, knowing they only came up and talked to you because of your face?" Dax sipped his wine and realized somewhere along the way, he'd actually relaxed. He was on a date with a nice, attractive woman and they had several things in common. It was comfortable ground. "You like football?"

"Sure. It's mindless, you know? Easy to follow."

He did know. That was why he liked it, too. Wakefield Media took 99 percent of his gray matter on a regular basis; it was fantastic to veg out on Sundays, the one day a week he didn't focus on work. "We should catch a game sometime."

Elise might very well be legit, too. Candy was exactly his type, almost to the letter. Dax's neck went a little hot. Wasn't that an interesting turnabout? People in general might not surprise him, but Elise almost never failed to.

"I'd like that." Candy smiled widely enough to display a mouthful of expensively capped teeth. "Tailgating is my favorite part. It's like a six-hour party every Saturday and Sunday."

Dax liked a good party. But *six-hour* parties... every Saturday *and* Sunday? "You watch college ball too?"

"I guess. Is that who plays on Sundays? I forget which one is which. I, um, actually don't watch the game most of the time." Laughing, she shook her head carefully so that strands of hair brushed her bare shoulders and drew attention to her cleavage simultaneously. It was impressive. And it was his turn to give her some signals in kind. He knew this dance well.

Candy's phone beeped. His was on silent, which he considered an unbreakable date rule. Obviously she didn't subscribe to it.

"Oh, pardon me," she tittered in that fake way designed to make it seem like an accident her phone wasn't off, when it was anything but. "I have to check in with my friend so she knows you didn't slip something in my drink and drag me ino a dark alley."

"No problem."

Okay, she got a pass on that one. It did make sense to be safe.

As she thumbed back a reply and then another one, Dax glanced at his own phone while his date texted with her girlfriend.

He had a couple of texts himself. As Candy was still facedown in her phone—likely sending messages to her female posse about Dax with the words "delish" and "rich" in all caps—he glanced at his own messages. They were both from Elise and, for some reason, that made him grin.

How's it going?

Must be going well since you're not answering.

His smile widened as he responded: She's great.

And left it at that. Elise could wait for her full report. While Candy finished texting what must be half the female population of Dallas, Dax sipped his wine and amused himself by imagining a certain matchmaker cooling her jets as she waited for additional details. Which he wasn't going to give her until he was good and ready.

Elise sat on her hands so she couldn't tap out a reply. Dax was on a date with Candy and she had no business bothering him with inane text messages.

But there was so much riding on this. Of all the women in her database, Candace Waters had the best shot at keeping Dax from vilifying Elise's company. Well, and obviously she wanted Candy to find the love of her life too. Dax was charming, sinfully hot even with his clothes on, and quick on the draw with that intelligent sense of humor.

What wasn't to like? If you were into that kind of man, which Candy totally should be.

But what if Dax didn't like Candy? "She's great" didn't really say a whole lot, but then they'd only just met. Elise had to give them both a chance to find out more about each other and trust the process that she herself had created.

To keep her hands busy, she tried typing up copy for an ad campaign that needed to go out immediately. January was just around the corner, which was traditionally a demanding time for EA International. The one-two punch of Christmas and then Valentine's Day got people motivated to find someone special.

Once Dax grilled Candy for all her personal history and figured out what she'd like, what kind of Christmas gift would he buy her?

Yeah, the ad copy wasn't working as a distraction either.

She grabbed her phone and texted Dax back: That's it? Great? Do you like her?

In agony, she stared at the phone waiting for the reply. Nothing.

Dax was ignoring her. On purpose. Not sending a message was as pointed a message as actually sending one.

Butt out, her blank screen said.

Now she really had to stop obsessing. She pushed the button to power off the phone and tossed it on the couch where she couldn't see it.

Maybe she should comb through some applications for her makeover program. Juliet had been such a challenge and then such a triumph, Elise hadn't taken on a new project yet. There were so many deserving applicants, from the one who'd been caring for her three younger brothers after the death of their parents, to another who'd been in the foster care system her whole life and just wanted to find someone who would love her forever.

Decision made, Elise sat down in her home office to contact them both. These two women had stayed on her mind for a reason, and she could handle two houseguests at the same time. Dannie would help out with the hair and makeup sessions, and after the infusion of cash from Prince Alain's match fee, Elise could afford to feed and clothe two women for a couple of months.

She never charged for her makeover services, instead choosing to gift these destitute women with new lives. Elise's magic wand might be the only opportunity they would have to succeed.

Done. She glanced at the time as she saved the

women's information to EA International's database using a remote connection. Eight whole minutes had passed.

Why was she so *antsy?*

Because she'd butchered Dax's profile questions the first time. What if she'd messed it up the second time and Candy wasn't really his soul mate?

Armed with a bowl of grapes and a tall glass of ice water, she opened the algorithm code, grimly determined to sort through how it had arrived at the original match so she could reasonably conclude if it had completed the second match correctly.

After fifteen minutes of wishing the grapes were chocolate and staring at code until her eyes crossed, she couldn't stand it. Retrieving her phone from its place of banishment, she powered it on. And powered it off before it fully booted up.

What was she doing? She might as well drive to the restaurant and peer through the window like a stalker. And worse, she had a feeling she might have done exactly that if she had a clue where Dax and Candy had met.

Ridiculous. She'd check for text messages once and then find a movie or something to watch.

She powered on the phone. Nothing.

That...*man*. She couldn't think of a bad enough word to encapsulate how infuriating Dax Wakefield was. He knew how much this meant to her. Knew she was on pins and needles. How hard would it have been to type, "She's beautiful and fun. I like her a lot"?

Not hard. He wasn't doing it because ignoring Elise was part of the game, to make her think the date was going from bad to worse, so she'd sit here and stew about losing.

In reality, he was laughing it up with Candy, having an awesome time drinking red wine and talking about their similar interests. Right now, he was probably watching her over his wineglass with those smoky bedroom eyes and somehow getting Candy to admit things she'd never told anyone before.

Maybe they'd moved to the parking lot and Dax had Candy cornered against her car, breathless and...that was going too far for a first date. They should be taking things slowly, not jumping right into something physical, the way Dax most assuredly did with all his previous women.

Immediately, Elise pulled up the text app: Candy doesn't go all the way on a first date.

She groaned. Dax had officially fried her brain. She hit the delete button.

Oh, God, had she just hit Send? *Please, please, please*, she prayed, hoping against hope she'd deleted the message as she'd meant to, and scoured her phone's folders for the answer.

Which she instead got in the form of a message from Dax: Speaking from personal experience?

Her stomach flopped at the same time she laughed, quite against her will. He'd made the faux pas okay and comical in one shot. How did he *do* that?

At least she'd gotten him to respond. She replied: You specified no one-night stands. She's in it for the long haul.

Dax: I wouldn't have called her otherwise.

That flopped her stomach in a different way. If this worked, Dax and Candy might very well get married. Most of the couples she matched did. She was in the business of introducing soul mates, after all.

Why did the thought of Dax and Candy falling blissfully in love make Elise want to cry?

The prospect of another round of holidays alone coupled with the stress of dealing with Dax—that was it. They were both killing her. Slowly.

And…if someone as cynical about relationships as Dax found his happily ever after, what did it say that she couldn't find hers?

Five

Candy laughed again and launched into another convoluted story about her dog. Dax was more than a little sorry he'd asked if she had any hobbies. Who knew a dog could be a hobby? Or that a grown woman would actually shop for outfits for said dog?

He signaled the bartender for another round and not for the first time, his attention wandered.

She finally wrapped up her monologue and leaned forward to give him an eyeful of her strategically exposed cleavage, which meant he wasn't paying enough attention to her. It was the fourth time she'd done it in thirty minutes, not that he was counting. Her signals were just so uncomplicated and easy to read.

Despite Elise's warning to the contrary, Candy was most definitely open to ending the night skin-on-skin. She would be energetic and creative in bed and yeah, it would be pleasurable.

But in the morning, she'd wake up intending to pursue a long-term, very serious relationship. Big difference from his usual dates. Regardless, he should embrace the spirit of what Elise had set up here, so when it failed, his conscience was clear.

Time to pay attention to his date. After all, she was supposed to be his soul mate. She certainly had a distinct lack of interest in what was going on behind his curtain. Likely she hadn't noticed he had one.

Giving Candy another practiced smile, he nodded to the door and stood, palm extended. "Shall we find a place to have a bite to eat?"

It was how these things worked—if drinks went well, you asked the woman to dinner. If not, you said you'd call her and escaped. Not that he'd claim drinks had gone particularly well, but maybe over dinner Candy would reveal some hidden depths he couldn't resist.

Without bothering to play coy, she took his hand

and slid off the bar stool, rising to her full height. "I'd love to."

Jeez, her legs were long. Too long. She was almost as tall as Dax.

"Pardon me while I powder my nose," she said, and turned to sway across the room with a one-two gait.

Dax was meant to think it was sexy. He *should* think it was sexy. But, all at once, nothing about Candy seemed sexy. The lady had moves and a clear interest in demonstrating them. She was exactly the type of woman he went for in a big way. Something was broken here.

His phone vibrated in his pocket, distracting him totally from Candy's departure. His lips curled up involuntarily. He pulled it out, expecting to see another text from Elise. Which it was.

I hope you're not checking your messages in front of Candy. Because that would be rude.

He laughed, painfully aware it was the first genuine amusement he'd felt all evening. He hit Reply: Then stop texting me.

Elise: .

He groaned through another laugh. A blank message. Her sense of humor slayed him.

Candy materialized in front of him far sooner than expected. "Ready?" she said.

"Sure." He pocketed his phone and followed his date out into the chilly night. She didn't have a coat, deliberately of course, so Dax could offer her his. Then she'd accidentally-on-purpose leave something in the pocket—lipstick, an earring; it varied from woman to woman—so she'd have an excuse to call him.

He shrugged out of his jacket anyway and handed it to her, earning a grateful smile as she slung it around her shoulders.

That's what he had to offer in a relationship—a coat. Nothing more. And it wasn't fair to Candy, who came into this date thinking there might be a possibility of something magical. The back of his neck heated. If Candy was his soul mate, she deserved better.

This was jacked up. He never should have called her. But how else could he have handled this? To prove Elise ran a sham business, he had to go on the date. Who knew said date would be exactly like every other date he'd ever been on, which had worked quite well for a long time, and yet not feel right?

As they walked to the valet stand, Candy stumbled, just a little and with practiced grace. Dax rolled his eyes even as he slung a steadying arm around her waist. She peered up at him in invitation. *Kiss me and let's get this party started,* she said without saying a word.

He could have scripted this date ahead of time and not missed a trick. Wearily, he eyed Candy's plumped lips, knew how good it would feel when she melted into him. On paper, they made sense together, for the short term anyway.

And he had no interest in her whatsoever. The perfect woman wasn't so perfect. What was *wrong* with him?

Elise was wrong with him. She'd set him up on a date with a woman who had all these long-term, soul-mate, mumbo-jumbo expectations and it was seriously cramping his style.

And okay, it pricked at his conscience too. Which had picked a fine time to surface.

Elise had ruined his ability to have fun on a date. She'd pay for that.

"I'm sorry, Candy, but this isn't going to work out."

"Oh." Candy straightened, her face hardening. "But we were matched. By Elise. I was really happy with her choice. But you're not?"

Obviously she'd not been clued in that this date was also part of an experiment. And a wager. Yet another mark against Elise.

"She did a great job matching us. You're exactly the kind of woman I like."

"Then what's the problem?"

"I'm not interested in a relationship, and it would be unfair to you for us to continue." The standard excuse rolled from his tongue.

"You forgot to say it's not you, it's me." Candy had obviously heard the excuse before too. She flung his jacket at him with surprising force. "Thanks for the drinks. Have a nice life."

She flounced to the valet and tapped her foot while the uniformed kid raced to get her car. Then she roared out of the parking lot with a screech.

Not only had Elise ruined him, she'd set him up in a catch-22. There was no way he could have fallen for Candy, not when it meant he'd lose the wager. Plus, all of Elise's profile questions kept getting in the way, making him think about his intentions. *That* was the problem, not the sound bite he'd spieled off to Candy.

The valet pulled Dax's car into the lane and hopped out. Dax slipped him a folded bill and got behind the wheel. The closer he drove to his loft, the deeper his blood boiled. Thanks to a certain matchmaker, he'd be spending yet another night alone, his least favorite thing to do.

He pulled onto a side street and hit the call button on his phone before checking the time. Almost nine.

Elise answered on the first ring, so he didn't worry about interrupting her plans too much.

"Expecting my call?" he said with as much irony as he could. She must have been sitting there watching her phone like a hawk. On a Friday night. Looked like Elise could use a bit of her own magic to find a date.

"Um, yeah," she said, her voice husky as though she'd been running laps, and it sent heat to his blood in a whole different way. "You said you'd give me the full report. Isn't this it?"

He'd totally forgotten about that, but it was absolutely the reason for his call now. "Text me your address. It's an in-person kind of report."

He ended the call and an instant later, the message appeared.

Who said I was at home?

She was *not* allowed to make him laugh when he was still so furious with her.

The address came through a moment later and

the grin popped out before he'd realized it. *Let's rock and roll, Ms. Arundel.*

Looked like he wouldn't be returning to his empty loft just yet after all.

Elise answered the door of her uptown condo wearing jeans and a soft yellow sweater, all perky and cupcake-y though she'd only had a few minutes' warning before Dax appeared on her front porch. He tried really hard to not notice how the sweater brought out gold highlights in her eyes. He was mad at her for…something.

"That was fast," she said and raised her eyebrows in that cool, infuriating way that said she had his number. "Did you observe the speed limit at any point on your way here?"

"Gonna give me a ticket?" He crossed his arms and leaned a shoulder on the door frame, because she'd very pointedly not invited him in. That was okay. The view was pretty good from here.

"No, a guess. The date must not have gone well if you were in that much of a hurry to get here."

"You think I wanted to see you instead?"

How had she arrived at that conclusion?

But then hadn't he compared Candy to Elise all night and never found a thing in Candy's favor?

Hadn't he anticipated this showdown with Elise during the drive over and looked forward to it far more than he'd anticipated having a naked Candy in his arms?

Well, it was stupid to pretend otherwise, regardless of how ridiculous it sounded. The facts spoke for themselves. He'd wanted to see Elise. He liked baiting her.

She stared at him as if he'd grown an extra nose. "No, ding-dong. Because you wanted to lord it over me that I didn't match you with your soul mate."

"Yeah." He nodded by rote and mentally kicked himself. *Ding-dong.* It might be funny if it wasn't so true. "That's why I sped over here. To tell you Candy was perfect, but it didn't work out."

Perfect for the man he'd shown Elise, anyway. She'd failed to dig beneath the surface and find the perfect woman for the man behind the curtain. *Not as good as you think you are, huh, Ms. Hocus-Pocus?*

Elise cocked her head, contemplating him. "I know she's perfect. I matched you with her. But you never really gave it a chance, did you?"

No point in pretending on that front. "What do you want me to say, Elise? I never made any bones about the fact that I'm not interested in a relationship."

No, that wasn't entirely true. He wasn't interested in a relationship with anyone he'd ever met and part of him was disappointed Elise hadn't pulled someone out of her hat who could change his mind.

But that would have been impossible because she didn't exist.

Dax sighed, weary all of a sudden. "Look, the idea of true love is as bogus as the idea of feeding a bunch of data into a program and expecting something magical to come out."

The porch light highlighted a strange shadow in her expression. "It's not magic. The algorithm is incredibly complex."

"I'm sure the software company told you that when they sold it to you but there's no way a developer can be that precise with intangibles. Admit it, you're—"

"I wrote the program," she interrupted, so softly he had strain to hear her.

Then the words sank in and he forgot all about getting her to admit the matches were actually just random pairings. "*You* wrote the program? You have a psychology degree."

The shadows deepened in her expression and he

felt like crap for opening his mouth without censor. He'd hurt her feelings, not once but twice. At what point had she started to care what he thought of her?

"I do have a psychology degree. A master's. My bachelor's degree is in computer science."

"A *master's?*"

"That's right." Her jaw tightened. "I almost went on for the PhD in psychology but decided to take the plunge with EA International instead. I can always go back to school later."

"But…you wrote the program?"

She might very well be the sharpest woman he'd ever met. And not just because she'd earned an advanced degree. Because she defied his expectations in ways he'd only begun to appreciate.

Her slight form held a wealth of secrets, things he'd never imagined might lie beneath the surface. Things he'd never dreamed would be so stimulating—intellectually *and* physically. After an incredibly frustrating night in the company of an inane woman who dressed dogs for fun, he wanted to uncover every fascinating bit of Elise Arundel.

"Is it *really* so hard to believe?" She crossed her arms, closing herself off from him. It was way past time for a heartfelt apology.

"It's not that I don't believe it, it's just so incredibly sexy." That was not even close to an apology and he needed to shut up, like yesterday. "I mean, I wasn't kidding. Brains turn me on."

Her eyebrows drew together. "Really? Because I have one in a jar on my kitchen counter. I've never found it particularly attractive but to each his own."

In a spectacularly unappealing combo, he snorted and laughed at the same time. "Wait. You're kidding, right?"

She rolled her eyes, but a suspicious tug at her lips told him she was having a hard time not laughing. "I do not now, nor have I ever, had a pickled brain in my possession."

"It was worth the clarification." A host of things unsaid passed between them, most of them indecipherable. He wanted to unscramble her in the worst way. "How bad is to admit that a conversation about pickled brains is the most scintillating one I've had this evening?"

With a sigh, Elise butted the door all the way open with the flat of her hand. "You better come in. I have a feeling I need to be sitting down for the full report."

Inside—exactly where he wanted to be, but not

to discuss Candy. Dax trailed the matchmaker through a classically decorated condo with rich, jewel-toned accents. "So this is where all the magic happens?"

"The women who go through my makeover program stay here, yes." Elise flopped on the sofa, clearly unconcerned about appearing graceful.

She had no pretense. It was almost as if she didn't care whether he found her attractive. She wasn't even wearing lipstick. The only time he'd ever seen a woman without lipstick was after he'd kissed it off. Women of his acquaintance always put their best face forward.

But Elise hadn't invited him in for any sort of behind-closed-doors activities. She wanted the lowdown on his date with another woman. This was like sailing through uncharted waters during a hurricane.

Slightly off stride, he sank into the plush armchair near the couch.

"Tell me what happened with Candy," she instructed without preamble. "Every last detail. I have to know precisely what didn't work, if anything did work, more abou—"

"Whoa. Why do you have to know all that?" That bug-on-cork feeling was back and on a Friday night in the company of an interesting woman, no variation of this conversation sounded like it would lead to the kind of fun he'd rather be having.

Her stare was nothing short of withering. "So I can get it right the second time."

"What second time?"

"I promised to match you with the love of your life. Admittedly, I like to get it right the first time, but I'm okay with one mistake. Two is unacceptable. So I need details."

Another date? He almost groaned. Somehow he'd thought they could let that lie, at least for a blessed hour or two. The wager was over. She'd lost. Didn't she realize that?

"Elise…"

She gazed across the coffee table separating them, and he couldn't do it. Couldn't denounce her as a fraud, couldn't tell her flat out that she wasn't the fairy godmother she seemed to think she was, couldn't stand the thought of hurting her feelings again.

Then there was the whole problem of this strange draw he felt every time he thought about Elise. Without this mission of hers to match him with his mythical soul mate, he'd have no excuse to see her again, and the thought made him twitchy.

She held up her hand in protest. "I know what you're going to say. You don't kiss and tell. I'm not asking you to."

"I didn't kiss Candy. And that wasn't what I was going to say."

"You didn't kiss her?" Elise looked a little shocked. "Why not?"

"Because I didn't like her. I only kiss women I like."

"But the other day at the bistro, you almost kissed *me*. I know you were about to. Don't bother to deny it."

As Dax did actually know the value of silence on occasion, he crossed his arms and waited until all the columns in her head added up. A blush rose on her cheeks. Really, he shouldn't enjoy that so much.

And he probably shouldn't have admitted he liked her. Not even to himself, but definitely not to her. Too late now.

"Stop being ridiculous," she said. "All this talk about how I'm sexy because I wrote a computer program and trying to throw me off balance with cryptic comments designed to make me believe you like me—it's not going to work."

She thought he was lying. Better yet, she thought

he'd told her those things for nefarious purposes, as a way to manipulate her, and she wanted to be clear there was no chance of her falling for it. If he hadn't liked her already, that alone would have clinched it, and hell if he knew why.

Thoroughly intrigued, he leaned forward, elbows on his knees. "What exactly am I working here?"

"The same thing you've been working since moment one. Distraction. If I'm all flustered and thinking about you kissing me, I'll mess up and match you with the wrong woman. Then I lose. It's brilliant, actually."

And instantly, he hit his stride. The wager, the full report he'd come to deliver, soul mates and matches—all of it got shoved to the back burner in favor of the gem buried in Elise's statement.

He zeroed right in on the kicker. "You're thinking about kissing me?"

Kissing Dax was, in fact, *all* Elise had been thinking about.

Did they make human muzzles? Because she needed one. "I said you were *trying* to get me to think about it. So I'd be distracted. It doesn't work."

Because she didn't need to think about kissing him to be distracted. That had happened the moment she'd opened the door to all that solid masculinity encased in a well-cut body. She didn't know for sure that he still had the washboard abs. But it was a safe bet. And it was easy to fantasize about when she already had a handy image emblazoned across her mind's eye of him half-naked.

Casually, Dax pulled at the sleeve of his date-night suit, which shouldn't have looked so different on him than what he'd worn all the other times she'd seen him. But it was clearly custom-made from gorgeous silk, and in it, he somehow he managed to look delicious and dangerous at the same time.

"Really," he said. It was a statement, not a question, as though he didn't believe her.

Probably because he knew she was skirting the truth. Why had she invited him in? Or given him her address in the first place? This was her sanctuary, and she rarely allowed anyone to intrude.

Dax got a pass because she *had* messed up. "You can't distract me. I've got a one-track mind and it's set on finding the perfect woman for you. Candy wasn't it. I get that. But her name came up due to the unorthodox profile sessions. We have to do the last one and do it the right way."

For all the good it would do. Who else did she

have in her database to match with Dax? Mentally, she sorted through the candidates and tried to do some of the percentages in her head.

And forgot how to add as a slow smile spread across his face, heavy with promise and a side of wicked. "Shall we put that to the test?"

"Um…" Her brain went a little fuzzy as he pierced her with those smoky eyes and raked heat through her abdomen without moving an inch. "Put what to the test?"

Then he stirred and she wished he'd stayed still.

He flowed to his feet and resettled next to her on the couch. "Whether I can distract you or not."

Barely a finger width separated them and she held her breath because oh my God, he smelled like sin and salvation and she had the worst urge to nuzzle behind his ear.

This was not part of the deal. She was *not* attracted to Dax Wakefield. It was unthinkable, unacceptable. She had no experience with a predatory man who had a new woman in his bed more often than he replaced his tube of toothpaste.

How could this have happened? Did her previously comatose libido not understand what a player this man was? How greatly he disdained long-term commitment and true love?

The man was her lonely heart's worst nightmare wrapped in a delectable package. She might as well hand him a mallet and lie down at his feet so he could get to smashing her insides flat right away.

He was meant for his true soul mate, who would be the right woman to change his mind about love. Elise was not it.

Pulse hammering, she stared him down, praying he couldn't actually see her panic swirling. Now would be a great time for some pithy comeback to materialize in her fuzzy brain, but then he slipped his hand under hers and raised it to his lips.

Her fingertips grazed his mouth and his eyelids drifted lower, as if he found it pleasurable. Fascinating. Little old Elise Arundel could make a walking deity like Dax feel pleasure. Who would have thought?

Watching her intently, he pursed his lips and sucked, ever so slightly, on her index finger, and the answering tug between her legs wasn't so slight. Honeyed warmth radiated outward, flushing over her skin, and a hitch in her lungs made it hard to catch a breath.

"What are you doing?" she asked hoarsely.

"Seeing what you taste like," he murmured and slid her hand across his stubbly jaw, holding it against his skin. "And it was good enough to want more."

Before she could blink, his head inclined and his lips trailed across hers, nibbling lightly, exploring, teasing, until he found what must have been the angle he sought. Instantly, their mouths fused into a ragingly hot kiss.

Elise's long-dormant body thundered to life and broke into a rousing rendition of the Hallelujah Chorus.

His hands cupped her neck, tilting her head back so he could take it deeper. Hot and rough, his tongue slicked across hers, and she felt strong responding licks deep in her core. A cry rose up in her throat and came out as a moan.

Those strong and deft hands drifted lower on her back, dipping under the hem of her sweater, spreading across her bare skin at the arch of her waist.

Stop right there.

He did.

She really wished he'd kept going.

They both shifted closer, twining like vines. Then he pushed with his palm against the small of her back and shoved her torso into his. Oh, my, it was hard against the roused tips of her breasts, which were sensitive enough to feel him through layers of cloth.

This wasn't the PG-rated kiss she'd been thinking about since the almost-kiss of the parking lot. This one had *rated R* slapped all over it. Fisting great wads of his shirt in her hands, she clung to him as he kissed her, shamelessly reveling in it, soaking up every second.

Until she remembered this was all designed as a distraction.

Pulling away was harder than it should have been. Chest rising and falling rapidly, she put a foot of couch between them. Not enough. She hit the floor and kept going, whirling only when the coffee table was between her and the hot-tongued man on the couch.

"Good kisser," she said breathlessly and cursed her fragmented voice. "I'll note it on your profile."

His heavy-lidded gaze tracked her closely. "I wasn't finished. Come back and see what else I'm good at. You want to be thorough on the profile, don't you?"

"I can't do that." If he triggered such a severe reaction with merely a kiss, what would her body do with more?

"Scared?"

"Of you? Not hardly." The scoff was delivered so convincingly, she almost believed it herself.

A light dawned in his expression and she had the distinct impression he'd just figured out exactly how much he scared her. That sent another round of panic into the abyss of her stomach.

"There's just no need," she clarified, desperately trying to counter the effects of being kissed sense-less. "We put it to the test, and while the kiss was pleasant, it certainly didn't distract me from the next steps. When do you want to schedule the last session?"

Dax groaned the way someone does when you tell them they have to get a root canal followed by a tax audit. "I'd rather kiss you some more. Why are you all the way over there?"

"We're not doing this, Dax. Hear me now, be-cause I can't stress this enough. You and I are not happening." She held up a finger as he started to speak. "No. Not any variation of you and I. We have a deal, a wager, and nothing more. I have to do my job. It's my life, my business. Let me do it."

He contemplated her for a long moment. "This is important to you."

"Of course it is! You threatened to destroy my reputation, which will effectively ruin the company

I've built over the last seven years. How would you like it if I had the power to do that to you and then spent all my time trying to seduce you into losing?"

"Elise." He waited until she glanced at him to continue. "I'm sorry. That was not my intent. I like kissing you. That's all. If you want to do another session, I'll be there. Name the time."

Oh, how *dare* he be all understanding and apologetic and smoky-eyed? "How about if I call you?"

She needed Dax gone before she did anything else stupid, like set off on an exploratory mission to see if he still had underwear-model abs under that suit.

"Sure. I can give you some space. Call me when you're ready to pick up where we left off."

Of course he'd seen right through her and then dumped a heck of a double entendre in her lap. Pick up where they left off with the sessions—or with the kiss? And which way would he interpret it?

Which way would she mean it?

She'd just realized something painful and ridiculous. The text messages during his date, letting him kiss her, the supreme sadness of imagining him blissfully in love with his soul mate; it all rolled up into an undeniable truth—she didn't want Dax to be with anyone else.

And she couldn't let herself be with him, even for what would undoubtedly be the best night of her life. It was the morning after when she woke up alone, knowing she hadn't been enough to keep him, and all the mornings alone from then on, that she couldn't do.

That was the best reason of all to get him matched with someone else in a big hurry.

Six

At precisely seven-thirty the next evening, Elise's doorbell rang. And yes, Dax was exactly who she expected to see grinning at her on the other side of the door, both hands behind his back.

"I said I'd call you."

Not that she'd really thought he'd wait around for the phone to ring, but he could have given her at least twenty-four hours to figure out how to call him without creating the impression she wanted him to pick up *exactly* where that kiss had left off.

Which would be really difficult to convey, when truthfully, she did. And now her house was spotless because every time she considered picking up the phone, she cleaned something instead.

"I know. But I'm taking this seriously. For real. Your office isn't the best place to get answers to your questions. So we're going to do it here."

"Here? At my house?" *Bad, bad idea.* "You want to do the profile session on a Saturday night?"

Didn't he have a new woman lined up already? Candy hadn't worked out, but a man like Dax surely wouldn't wait around for Elise to find him some action. Saturday night equaled hot date, didn't it?

"I don't think you fully appreciated the point I made about getting to know me best while on a date." With a flourish, he pulled something from behind his back. A DVD she didn't recognize. "So we're going to watch a movie."

"The profile session is going to be a date?" *She* was his hot date. How in the world had she not seen this coming?

It was straight out of Psych 101—to get the cheese, she had to complete the maze. But why? What was his motivation for forcing her to navigate a date in the first place?

"More of a compromise," he allowed with a nod. "This is not anything close to what I've ever done on a date. But the setting is innocuous and we can both relax. I don't feel like you're grilling me, you don't feel like it's work."

That sounded remarkably like the excuse he'd used to get her to go to lunch, which had proved to be rather effective, in retrospect. "What if I'm busy?"

"Cancel your plans. You want to know what makes me tick?" His eyebrows lifted in invitation. "I'm offering you a shot. Watch the movie. Drink some wine. If you do that for me, I'll answer any question you ask honestly."

Dax gestured with his other hand, which clutched a bottle of cabernet sporting a label she'd only ever seen behind glass at a pricey restaurant.

She shook her head. "This is a thinly veiled attempt to seduce me again."

The sizzling once-over he treated her to should not have curled her toes. Of course, if he'd given her a warning before he showed up, she could have put on shoes.

"I'm not trying to tilt the scales by coming on to you," he insisted. "Trust me, if I wanted you naked, this is not how I would go about it."

As she well knew his seduction routine, she opted to keep her mouth shut. For once.

"I, Daxton Wakefield, will not touch you one

single time this whole evening." He marked the statement by crossing his heart solemnly with the DVD case. "Unless you ask me to."

"You're safe on that front. Not that I'm agreeing to this, but what did you bring?" She nodded at the movie against her better judgment.

He shrugged. "An advanced screening copy of *Stardate 2215*. It's that big-budget sci-fi flick coming out Christmas day."

She eyed him. "That's not in theaters yet. How did you get a copy?"

"I have friends in low places." He grinned mischievously. "One of the benefits of being in the media business. I called in a few favors. You like sci-fi and I wanted to pick something I knew you hadn't seen."

Speechless, she held on to the door so she didn't end up in a heap at his feet. She'd never told him what kind of movies she liked, but somehow he'd figured it out, and then went to great lengths to get one. Her heart knocked up against her principles and it was not cool.

Not a seduction, my foot.

But she really wanted to see that movie. And she really wanted to get Dax Wakefield matched to someone else so she could stop thinking about kissing him.

"Truce?" He held out the DVD and the wine with a conciliatory smile and he looked so freaking gorgeous in his $400 jeans and long-sleeved V-neck, she wanted to lap him up like whipped cream.

If that bit of absurdity didn't decide against this idea for her, nothing would.

"I haven't eaten dinner yet."

"Jeez, Elise." He huffed out a noise of disgust. "You're the most difficult woman to not have a date with in the entire United States. Order a pizza. Order twelve. You may have free rein with my credit card if that's what it takes to get me over your threshold."

"Why are you so dead-set on this? Honestly."

He dropped his arms, wine and DVD falling to his sides. "Believe it or not, this is me leveling the field. You deserve a genuine chance at doing your thing with the questions and the algorithm. This is an atmosphere conducive to giving you that."

Sincerity laced his words, but to clarify, she said, "Because you don't like my office."

Something flitted through his expression and whatever it was scared her a great deal more than the kiss. "Because I have an extremely full week ahead and daylight hours are scarce. I want to give you my undivided attention, without watching the clock."

Her heart knocked again.

"You've just won an evening with a match-maker." She stepped out of the door frame and allowed Dax passage into the foyer for the second time in two days.

She should have her head examined.

True to his word, he strolled past her without touching, went to the living room and set the wine on the coffee table.

She fetched wineglasses and he ordered the pizza. They settled onto the couch and three sips in, she finally relaxed. "This cabernet is amazing. Where did you find it?"

"In my wine rack." He handed her the remote without grazing her fingers. It was carefully done. "I was saving it for a special occasion."

"Right. Pizza and a movie is special."

He didn't move, didn't touch her at all, but she felt the look he gave her in all the places his kiss had warmed the night before. "The company is the occasion, Elise."

Prickles swept across her cheeks. The curse of the fair-skinned Irish. She might as well take out a billboard proclaiming her innermost thoughts. "We'll get through the profile session much faster if you quit detouring to flatter me with platitudes."

His head tilted as if he'd stopped to contemplate a particularly intriguing Picasso. "Why do you find it so hard to believe that I like you?"

Because he made a habit of working emotions to his advantage. Because he was a swan and she was not. Because to believe would be akin to trusting him.

But she ignored all that in favor of the most important reason. "You don't ruin the reputation of someone you hold in fond regard. If you really like me, prove it. Let's end this now."

"To be fair, I didn't know I was going to like you when I made that deal. But if you do your job, you've got nothing to worry about, do you?" He lifted his glass in a mock toast.

A part of her had hoped he'd take the opportunity to call it off, and she shouldn't be so disappointed he hadn't. Why—because she'd internalized his pretty words? Thought maybe he'd realized she was actually a very nice person and hadn't deliberately set out to ruin his friendship with Leo?

"Hey."

"Hey, what?" she said a touch defensively, pretty sure she had no call to be snippy.

"It's a compliment that I'm holding fast to our deal. You're a smart, savvy woman and if I didn't respect the hell out of you, I'd have let you bow out long before now."

"Bow out? You mean give up and quit? No way."

When he grinned, she deflated a little. He'd phrased it like that on purpose to get her dander up and allow him to slide the nice stuff by her. How did he know how to handle her so well?

"That's why I like you," he said decisively. "We're both fighters. Why else would I be here to put myself through your profile wringer? I can't claim the matchmaking process is bogus unless I submit to it wholly. Then we both know the victor deserves to win."

Now he'd dragged ethics into this mess. She shook her head in disbelief. Against all odds, she liked him too.

Somehow he'd stripped everything away and laid out some very profound truths. Of all the ways he could have convinced her he really liked her, how had he done it by *not* calling off their deal?

He respected her skills, respected her as a business woman, and she'd been on the defensive since moment one. It was okay to let her guard down. Dax had more than earned it.

"It's hard for me to trust people," she said slowly, watching him to see if he had a clue how difficult a confession this was. "That's why I give you so much grief."

He nodded once without taking his eyes off her. "I wasn't confused. And for the record, same goes."

He stretched his hand out in invitation and she didn't hesitate to take it. Palm to palm, silent mutual agreement passed between them. Warmth filled her as the intensity of the moment unfolded into something that felt like kinship.

Neither of them trusted easily, but each of them had found a safe place here in this circle of two. At least for tonight.

Dax stopped paying the slightest bit of attention to the movie about fifteen minutes in. Watching Elise was much more fun.

She got into the movie the same way she did everything else—with passion. And it was beautiful. He particularly liked the part where she forgot they were holding hands.

There was nothing sexual about it. He didn't use it as an excuse to slide a suggestive fingertip across her knuckle. He didn't yank on her hand and let her spill into his lap, even though nothing short of amnesia was going to get that hot kiss out of his head.

Far be it from him to disrupt the status quo. The status quo was surprisingly pleasant. He'd agreed not to come on to her, and he'd stick to it, no matter how many more times she gave him a hard-on just by looking at him.

Promises meant something to him and he wanted Elise to understand that.

And oddly enough, when he knew there wasn't a snowball's chance for anything above pizza and a movie, it was liberating in a way he'd never expected.

It was new. And interesting. Instead of practicing his exit strategy, he relaxed and enjoyed the company of a beautiful woman who made him laugh. He couldn't wait to find out what happened next.

The pizza arrived, and he let her hand slip from his without protest, but his palm cooled far too quickly.

Elise set the box on the coffee table and handed Dax a bright red ceramic plate. The savory, meaty smell of pepperoni and cheese melded with the fresh-baked crust and his stomach rumbled. Neither of them hesitated to dig in.

Dax couldn't remember ever eating with a woman in front of the TV. It was something couples did. And he'd never been part of one. Never wanted to be, and furthermore, never wanted to give someone the impression there'd be more couple-like things to come.

But this wasn't a date and Elise wasn't going to get the wrong idea. It was nice.

"Thanks for the pizza," she said around a mouthful, which she couldn't seem to get down her throat fast enough. "I never eat it and I forgot how good it is. You do amazing things with a credit card."

She'd meant it as a joke but it hit him strangely and he had a hard time swallowing the suddenly tasteless bite in his own mouth.

Yes, his bank account could finance a small country, and he made sure the women he dated benefited from his hard work, usually in the form of jewelry or the occasional surprise overnight trip to New York or San Francisco. He'd never given it much thought.

Until now. What *did* he have to offer a woman in a relationship? A coat and a credit card. Thanks to his friendly neighborhood matchmaker, it seemed shallow and not…enough. What if Elise did the impossible and introduced him to his soul mate?

She was smart and had a good track record. She could actually pull it off.

By definition, his soul mate would be that woman worth making lifelong promises to.

Did he really want to meet her and be so inadequately prepared?

"You're supposed to be asking me questions." Dax gave up on the pizza and opted to drown his sudden bout of relationship scruples with more wine.

Eyebrows raised, Elise chewed faster.

"I suppose I am," she said and washed down the last of her pizza with a healthy swallow of cabernet, then shot him a sideways glance. "Say, you're pretty good. I did forget about work, just like you predicted."

He crossed his arms so he didn't reach for her hand again. It bothered him that he wanted to in the same breath as bringing up the profile questions designed to match him with another woman. "Yeah, yeah, I'm a genius. Ask me a question."

After pausing the movie, Elise sat back against the sofa cushion, peering at him over the rim of her glass. "What does contentment look like?"

This. His brain spit out the answer unchecked. Thankfully, he kept it from spilling out of his mouth. "I spend my day chasing success. I've never strived for contentment."

Which didn't necessarily mean he hadn't found it.

"What if Wakefield Media collapsed tomorrow but you had that woman next to you, the one who doesn't care about what's behind your curtain? Would you still be able to find a way to be content as long as you had her?"

No surprise that Elise remembered what he'd said at lunch the other day. How long would it take her to figure out he actually *wanted* someone to care?

Nothing was going to happen to Wakefield Media. It was hypothetical, just like the soul mate. So if this was all theoretical, why not have both?

"What if having the woman *and* success makes me content? Is that allowed?"

Somehow, the idea buried itself in his chest and he imagined that woman snuggled into his bed at the end of a long day, not because he'd brought her home, but because she lived there. And they were together but it wasn't strictly for sex—it was about emotional support and understanding—and making love heightened all of that.

Dax could trust she'd stick around. Forever.

"If that's what contentment looks like to you, then of course."

Her catlike smile drove the point home. She'd gotten a response out of him even though he'd have sworn he'd never so much as thought about how to define contentment.

He had to chuckle. "Well played."

Now that he'd defined it, the image of that woman wouldn't dissolve. She didn't have a face or a body type, but the blurred shape was there in his mind and he couldn't shake it.

What was he supposed to do with that?

With a nod at his concession, Elise sipped her wine and contemplated him. "What do you do with your free time?"

Dax grinned and opted to bite back the inappropriate comment about his after-hours activities. "Should I pick something that makes it sound like I have an interesting hobby?"

"No, you should say what you like."

"I like to people-watch," he said.

"Tell me more about that. What's great about people-watching?"

"Spoken in true therapist fashion." He meant it as a joke and she took it as one. He liked amusing her, and it was easy to do so. "People-watching is the best way to figure out what motivates the masses. And it never gets old."

She was really, really good at this, especially when he wasn't trying to weasel his way out of having his psyche split open. Actually, she had a knack for yanking things out of his brain even when he *was* looking for a way to avoid answering her questions.

So there was no point in being anything less than honest. Plus, this environment, this bubble with only the two of them, created a sort of haven, where it didn't seem so terrible to say whatever he felt.

"Go on," she encouraged with a small wave. "Why do you have to figure out what motivates people?"

"Wakefield Media isn't just a top-grossing media company. It's a top-grossing company, period. That's not an accident. I got a degree in psychology instead of business because it's crucial to have a keen understanding of what brings people back for more, especially in the entertainment space."

Wine and pizza totally forgotten, she listened with rapt attention as if he'd been outlining the secrets of the universe, which she couldn't get enough of. "And people-watching helps?"

For a woman who'd moaned so appreciatively over the pizza, she had amazing willpower. She'd only eaten one piece. She was so interested in what he said, food took a backseat. It was a little heady to be worthy of so much focus.

"People can be notoriously loyal to certain shows, and conversely, very fickle. You'd be shocked at how much you can pick up about why when you just sit and observe how people interact."

Her soft smile punched him in the gut. "Your insights must be something else."

"I bet yours would be as good. Do it with me some time."

Now why had he gone and said that? Hadn't he gotten a big enough clue that she didn't want to hang out with him? Look how hard it had been to get her to agree to pizza and a movie.

The wine must be messing with his head.

"I'd like that. It's a date," she said without a trace of sarcasm and he did a double take.

The wine was messing with her head too, obviously.

"A date that's not a date because we're not dating?" She'd been undeniably clear about that last night. Otherwise, he'd never have agreed to keep his hands off of her.

And look what that promise had netted him— this was bar none the most enjoyable evening he'd had in ages, including the ones that did involve sex.

"Right. We're not dating. We're...friends?" she offered hesitantly.

A denial sprang to his lips and then died. *Friends.* Is that what was happening here? Did that explain why he felt as though he could tell Elise anything?

"I don't know. I've never been friends with a woman. Aren't there rules?"

She made a face. "Like we're not supposed to cancel our plans with each other when someone we *are* dating calls?"

"Like I'm not supposed to fantasize about kissing you again." The answering heat in her expression told him volumes about her own fantasies. "Because if that's against the rules, I can't be friends with you."

She looked down, that gorgeous blush staining her cheeks. "You're not supposed to be doing that anyway. Regardless."

He tipped up her chin and forced her to meet his eyes again because that heat in hers liquefied him. And he craved that feeling only she could produce. "I can't stop."

As he'd just broken his promise not to touch her,

he tore his hand away from her creamy skin with reluctance and shoved it under his thigh.

Elise messed with his head. No wine required.

She blinked, banking all the sexy behind a blank wall. "You'll find it surprisingly easy to stop as soon as I match you with someone else. She'll help you forget all about that kiss, which never should have happened in the first place."

There it was again, slapping him in the face. Elise wasn't interested in him. Her main goal was to get him paired off with someone else as soon as possible.

And that was the problem. He didn't want to be matched with another Candy. The thought of another date with another woman who was perfect for him on paper but not quite right in reality...he couldn't do it.

He wanted that blurred woman snuggled into his bed, ready to offer companionship, understanding. Contentment. Instantly, she snapped into focus, dark hair swinging and wearing nothing but a gorgeous smile.

Elise.

Yes. He wanted Elise, and when Dax Wakefield wanted something, he got it.

But if he pursued her, would this easiness between them fall apart? After all, she wasn't his soul mate and that in and of itself meant she couldn't be that woman in his imagination, with whom he could envision a future.

What a paradox. He'd finally arrived at a place in his life where he could admit he'd grown weary of the endless revolving door of his bedroom. And the woman he pictured taking a longer-term spot in his bed wanted to be *friends,* right after she hooked him up with someone else. Whom he did not want to meet.

Where did that leave the wager between them?

Seven

Bright and early Monday morning, Elise sat in her office and plugged the last of the data into the system. Dax had answered every single question and she firmly believed he'd been honest, or at least as honest as he knew how to be when the content involved elements a perpetual player hardly contemplated. But they'd stayed on track Saturday night—mostly—and finished the profile. Finally.

This would be her hour of victory. She'd built a thriving business using nothing but her belief in true love and her brain. Not one thin dime had come from Brenna, and Elise had fought hard to keep herself afloat during the lean years. She would not let all her work crumble.

She was good at helping people find happiness. Matching Dax with someone who could give him that would be her crowning achievement.

She hit Run on the compiler.

Elise Arundel.

Her forehead dropped to the keyboard with a spectacular crash. She couldn't decide whether to laugh or cry.

Of course her name had come up again. The almost-kiss had been enough to skew the results the first time. Now she had a much bigger mess on her hands because she couldn't get the *oh-my-God* real kiss off her mind. Or the not-a-date with Dax, which should have only been about completing the profile, but instead had eclipsed every evening Elise had ever spent with a man. Which were admittedly few.

They'd bonded over pizza and mutual distrust. And—major points—he'd never made a single move on her. When he confessed he still thought about kissing her, it had been delivered with such heartbreaking honesty, she couldn't chastise him for it.

But his admission served as a healthy reminder. Dax liked women and was practiced at getting them. That's why it felt so genuine—because it was. And once he got her, she'd start dreaming of white dresses while he steadily lost interest. They were *not* a good match.

It didn't stop her from thinking about kissing him in return.

Her mixed feelings about Dax had so thoroughly compromised her matchmaking abilities she might as well give up here and now. It wasn't as though she could fiddle around with the results this time, not when it was so clear she couldn't be impartial. Not after Dax had made such a big deal about ethics.

She groaned and banged her head a couple more times on the keyboard. He was going to have a field day with this. Even if she explained that matchmaking was as much an art as a science, which was why she administered the profile sessions herself, he'd cross his arms and wait for her to confess this matchmaking business was bogus.

But it wasn't, not for all her other clients. Just this one.

The truth was, she abhorred the idea of Dax being matched with another woman so much, she'd subconsciously made sure he wouldn't be. It was unfair to his soul mate—who was still out there somewhere—and unfair to Dax. He was surprisingly sweet and funny and he deserved to be with a woman he could fall in love with. He deserved to be happy.

And she was screwing with his future. Not to mention the future of EA International, which would be short-lived after Dax crucified her matchmaking skills. That would be exactly what *she* deserved.

How in the world could she get out of this?

A brisk knock on her open door startled her into sitting up. Angie poked her head in, and the smirk on her assistant's face did not help matters.

"Mr. Wakefield is here," she said, her gaze cutting to the lobby suggestively.

"Here?" Automatically, Elise smoothed hair off her forehead and cursed. Little square indentations in the shape of keys lined her skin. "As in, here in the office?"

Maybe she could pretend to be out. At least until the imprint of the keyboard vanished and she figured out what she was going to tell him about his match. Because of course that was why he'd jetted over here without calling. He wanted a name.

"I've yet to develop hologram technology," Dax said smoothly as he strolled right past Angie, filling the room instantly. "But I'm working on it. In the meantime, I still come in person."

Hiding a smile but not very well, Angie made herself scarce.

Elise took a small private moment to gorge herself on the visual panorama of male perfection before her. She'd been so wrong. His everyday suit was anything but ordinary and he was as lickable in it as he was in everything else. And then her traitorous brain reminded her he was most lickable *out* of everything else.

Her mouth incredibly dry, she croaked, "I thought you were busy this week. That's what pizza was all about, right?"

He didn't bother with the chair intended for guests. Instead, he rounded the desk and stopped not a foot from her, casually leaning against the wood as if he owned it.

"I am. Busy," he clarified, his gaze avidly raking over her, as if he'd stumbled over a Van Gogh mural amid street graffiti and couldn't quite believe his luck. "I left several people in a conference room, who are this very minute hashing out an important deal without me. I got up and walked out."

For a man who claimed his company was more

important than anything, even contentment, it seemed an odd thing to do. "Why?"

His smoky irises captured hers and she fell into a long, sizzling miasma of delicious tension and awareness.

"I wanted to see you," he said simply.

Her heart thumped once and settled back into a new rhythm where small things like finding his real soul mate didn't matter. The wager didn't matter. The rest of her life alone didn't matter. Only the man mattered.

And he wanted to be with her.

"Oh. Well, here I am. Now what?"

He extended his hand in invitation. "I haven't been able to think about anything other than sitting on a park bench with you and watching the world go by. Come with me."

Her chair crashed against the back wall as she leaped up. She didn't glance at the clock or shut her computer down, just took his hand and followed him.

Most men took her hints and left her alone, more than happy to let her stew in her trust issues. Not this one. Thank goodness. She could worry about how wrong they were for each other and how she had to find someone right for him later.

Fall nipped the air and Elise shivered as she and Dax exited the building. Her brain damage apparently extended to braving the elements in a lightweight wool dress and boots.

"Hang on a sec. I need to go back and get my coat."

She turned when Dax spun her back. "Wait. Wear mine."

Shrugging out of his suit jacket, he draped it around her shoulders and took great care in guiding her arms through the sleeves. Then he stood there with the lapels gripped in his fists, staring down at her as if the act of sharing his warmth had great significance.

"You didn't have to do that," she said as she rolled up the sleeves self-consciously. But she had to do something with her hands besides put them square on his pectorals as she wanted to. "My coat is right in—"

"Humor me. It's the first time I've given a woman my coat because she needed it. I like it on you."

"I like it on me, too." She hunched down in it, stirring up that delicious blend of scent that was Dax, danger and decadence all rolled into one. She could live in this jacket, sleep in it, walk around naked with the silk liner brushing her skin...

Too bad she'd have to give it back.

They strolled down the block to the small urban park across the street from EA International's office building. Dax told her a funny story about a loose dog wreaking havoc at one of his news station studios and she laughed through the whole thing. Their hands brushed occasionally and she pretended she didn't notice, which was difficult considering her pulse shot into the stratosphere with every accidental touch.

She kept expecting him to casually take her hand, as he'd done Saturday night. Just two people holding hands, no big deal. But he didn't.

No wonder her feelings were so mixed. She could never figure out what to expect. For a long time, she'd convinced herself he only came on to her so she'd lose the wager. Now she wasn't so sure.

Dax indicated an unoccupied bench in the central area of the park, dappled by sunlight and perfectly situated to view a square block of office buildings. People streamed to and from the revolving doors, talking to each other, checking their phones, eyeing the traffic to dart across the street.

She'd opted to sit close, but not too close, to Dax. At least until she understood what this was all about. They might have bonded over the fact that neither of them trusted easily, but that didn't mean she'd developed any better ability to do so.

"How does this people-watching deal go?" She nodded at the beehive of activity around them.

He shrugged. "Mostly I let my mind wander and impressions come to me. Like that couple."

She followed his pointed finger to the youngish boy and girl engaged in a passionate kiss against the brick wall of a freestanding Starbucks.

"Eighteen to twenty-five," he mused. "Likely attending the art school around the corner. They both own smartphones but not tablets, have cable TV but not the premium channels, read Yahoo news but not the financial pages, and can tell me the titles of at least five songs on Billboard's Top 100, but not the names of any politicians currently in office except the president."

Mouth slightly agape, she laughed. "You made all that up."

Dax focused his smoky eyes on her instead of the couple and the temperature inside his jacket neared thermonuclear. "He has a bag with the art school logo and they both have phones in their back pockets. The rest is solid market research for that age group. The details might be slightly off, but not the entertainment habits."

"Impressive. Do you ever try to find out if you're right?"

He gave her a look and stretched his arm across the back of the bench, behind Elise's shoulders. "I'm not wrong. But feel free to go ask them yourself."

Carefully, she avoided accidentally leaning back against his arm. Because she wanted to. And didn't have any clue how to navigate this unexpected interval with Dax, or what to think, what to feel.

"Uh..." The couple didn't appear too interested in being interrupted and all at once, she longed to be that into someone, where the passing world faded from existence. "That's okay."

His answering smile relaxed her. Marginally.

Unfortunately, she had a strong suspicion she could get that into Dax.

"Your turn," he said. "What do you see in those two?"

Without censor, she spit out thoughts as they came to her.

"They're at an age where love is still exciting but has the potential to be that much more painful because they're throwing themselves into it without reservation. They're not living together yet, but headed in that direction. He's met her parents but she hasn't met his, because he's from out of state, so it's too expensive to go home with a girl unless it's serious. Next Christmas he'll invite her," she allowed. "And he'll propose on New Year's because it's less predictable than Christmas Eve."

Dax's lips pursed. "That's entirely conjecture."

He was going to make her work for it, just as she'd done to him.

"Is not. He has on a Choctaw Casino T-shirt, which is in Oklahoma, and if they lived together, they'd be at home, kissing each other in private. The rest is years of studying couples and what drives them to fall in love." She recoiled at the smirk on his face. "So, you can cite research but I can't?"

"Cite research all you want. *Validated* research." As he talked, he grew more animated and angled toward her. "You can't study how people fall in love. Emotions are not quantifiable."

"Says the guy with a psychology degree. How did Skinner determine that mice responded more favorably to partial reinforcement? Not by asking them whether they prefer Yahoo or Google news."

A grin flashed on his face and hit her with the force of a floodlight.

She fought a smile of her own and lost. "You

study, you make a hypothesis, you test it and *voilà*. You have a certified conclusion."

Only with Dax could she enjoy a heated argument about her first and only love, the science of the heart.

"So tell me, Dr. Arundel." His gaze swept her with some of that heat in a pointed way she couldn't pretend to miss. "What's your hypothesis about me? Break me down the way you did that couple."

The honks and chattering people filled the sudden silence as she searched his face for some clue to what he was after. Besides the obvious. Clearly he was still thinking about kissing her.

And she was pretty sure she wouldn't utter one single peep in protest.

Great. If she couldn't trust him and she couldn't trust herself to remember why they wouldn't work, why was she still sitting here in the presence of a master at seduction?

"Honestly?" He nodded but she still chose her words carefully. "You don't like to be alone, and women fill that gap. You want her to challenge you, to make it worth your while to stick around, which never happens, so you break it off before she gets too attached. It's a kindness, because you don't really want to hurt her. It's not her fault she's not the one."

His expression didn't change but something unsettled flowed through the depths of his eyes.

"What makes you think I'm looking for the one?" he said lightly. But she wasn't fooled. His frame vibrated with tension.

She'd hit a nerve. So she pressed it, hard.

"You never would have agreed to be matched if you weren't. And you certainly wouldn't keep coming back, especially after it didn't work out with Candy."

He shifted and their knees nested together suggestively. Slowly, he reached out and traced the line of her jaw, tucking an errant lock of hair behind her ear, watching her the entire time.

"I came for the match and stayed for the matchmaker."

"Dax, about that—"

"Relax."

His fingers slid through her hair, threading it until he'd reached the back of her neck. She was supposed to *relax* when he touched her like that?

"You're off the hook," he murmured. "I'm officially calling off our wager. Don't be disappointed."

He'd read her mind. Again.

Relief coursed through her body, flooding her so swiftly, she almost cried. She didn't have to confess that she'd skewed the results. He'd never have to know she'd abandoned her ethics.

But without the wager in place, she had no shield against the onslaught of Dax. No excuse to hold him at arm's length. Much, *much* worse, she had no excuse to continue their association.

"You don't think I can match you?"

"I think you can sell ice to Eskimos. But the fact of the matter is I don't want to meet any more women."

"But you have to," she blurted out. If he didn't, how would he ever meet the love of his life? She might have abandoned her ethics, but not the belief that everyone deserved to be deliriously happy.

Calmly, Dax shook his head. "I *don't* have to. I've already met the one I want. You."

A thousand nonverbal sentiments pinged between them, immobilizing her.

She wasn't right for him. He wasn't right for her. They didn't make sense together and she couldn't let herself think otherwise. Not even for a moment. The best way to stop wishing for things that couldn't be was to match him with someone else, wager or no wager. Then he could be happy.

Elise froze and forcibly removed his hand from her silky hair.

Now that was a shame. He liked the feel of her.

"Me?" she squeaked.

"Come on. Where did you think I was headed?" Apparently, telling a woman you wanted to see her wasn't enough of a clue that you were into her. "It would be a travesty to continue this matchmaking deal when it's not going to happen."

"What's not going to happen? Finding you a match?" Indignation laced her question.

But then he'd known she wouldn't go down without a fight. He'd have been disappointed otherwise. It had taken him most of Sunday to figure out how to maneuver past all her roadblocks. He still wasn't sure if he'd hit on the right plan. Chances were, she'd drop a few more unanticipated blockades.

That's what made it great.

"The concept was flawed from the beginning. And we both know it. Why not call a spade a spade and move on? We've got something between us." He held up a finger to stem the flow of protests from her mouth. "We do. You can't deny it. Let's see what happens if we focus on that instead of this ridiculous wager."

"I already know what's going to happen." A couple of suits walked by and she lowered her voice. "You'll take me to bed, it'll be glorious and you'll be insufferably smug about it. Hit repeat the next night and the next, for what...about three weeks?"

He bit back a grin. "Or four. So what's the problem?"

His grin slipped as she sighed painfully. "That's not what I want."

"You'd rather I fumble around with no clue how to find your G-spot and then act like it's okay when I come before you? Because I grew out of that before I hit my twenties. The smug part might be a little insufferable, but..." He winked. "I think you'll forgive me."

"You know what I'm saying, Dax. Don't be difficult."

He was being difficult?

"You want promises right out of the gate?" His temper flared and he reined it in. "I don't operate like that. No one does."

"Not promises. Just an understanding that we have the same basic goals for a relationship."

He groaned. "This is not a computer program

where you get to see the code before executing it. Why can't we take it day by day? Why can't it be like it was Saturday night?" His thumb found the hollow of her ear again. He spread his fingers against her warm neck and she didn't slap his hand away. "Today is pretty good, too. Isn't it?"

Her eyes shut for a brief moment. "Yeah. It's nice. But we want different things and it's not smart to start something when that hasn't changed. Am I supposed to give up the hope for a committed, loving relationship in exchange for a few weeks of great sex?"

"Who said you have to give up anything? Maybe you're going to gain something." A lot of something if he had his way. He waggled his brows. "What have you got against great sex?"

"I'm a fan of great sex, actually." She crossed her legs, pulling herself in tighter. "It's especially great when I can count on it to be great for a long time instead of wondering when the end is coming."

"Let's break down precisely what it is that you want, shall we?" His head tilted as he contemplated the slight woman who'd had him on the edge of his seat since day one. "You want desperately to find your soul mate but when a guy isn't exactly what you envisioned, you run screaming in the other direction. There's no middle ground."

Her fair skin flushed red. "That's not true."

It was, and she needed someone real to get her over her hang-ups and visions of fantasy lovers dancing in her head. "You have check boxes in your mind, profile questions that you want answered a certain way before you'll go for it. No guy could ever perfectly fit the mold. So you stay home on Saturday nights and bury yourself in futuristic worlds to avoid finding out your soul mate doesn't exist."

"Soul mates do exist! I've seen it."

"For some people." It was a huge reversal for him to admit that much, and she didn't miss it. "But maybe not for me, or for you. Did you ever think of that?"

"Never. Every male I've ever met, that's the first thing I wonder. Is he my soul mate?"

Every male? Even him? "But you don't take that first step toward finding out."

"Just as you evaluate every woman to see if she's the one, decide she can't be, and then don't stick around long enough to let her disappoint you."

Deflection. They were both pretty well versed in it when the subject material grew too hot, and digging into the fact that no one ever measured up—for either of them—was smoking. Escaping unsinged seemed more and more unlikely. But neither of them had jumped out of the fire yet.

She was scared. He got that. It squeezed his chest, and what was he supposed to do with that? After all, *he* was the one who scared her.

"Yeah," he allowed. "But I'm willing to admit it. Are you?"

She slumped down in his jacket, which almost swallowed her. Her wry smile warmed him tremendously. She looked so sweet and delectable sitting there wearing a jacket she hadn't tried to manipulate her way into, and an urgent desire to strip her out of it built with alarming speed.

"It's not fair, you know," she complained. "Why can't you be just a little stupid?"

He laughed long and hard at that and didn't mind that she'd evaded his challenge. He already knew the answer anyway.

"I should ask you the same thing. If you'd relax your brain for a minute, we could avoid all this."

"Avoid what? Psychoanalyzing each other under the table?"

"Hell no. That's the part about us that turns me on the most."

"There's no us," she said and looked away. Her cheeks flushed again, planting the strangest desire to put his lips on that pink spot. "What happened to being friends?"

"Would it make things easier for you to stick a label on this thing between us? I'm okay with calling us friends if you are. But be prepared for an extra dose of friendliness."

She snorted. "Let's skip the labels."

"Agreed. With all the labels off the table, let's just see what happens if I do this."

He tipped her chin up and drew her lips close, a hairbreadth from his, letting her get used to the idea before committing.

Her whole body stilled.

He wanted Elise-on-Fire, as she'd been on the couch the first time he'd kissed her, before she freaked out. And he felt not one iota of remorse in pushing her buttons in order to get her there.

"Scared?" he murmured against her lips. "Wanna go home and watch *Blade Runner* for the four-thousandth time?"

"Not with you," she shot back, grazing his mouth as she enunciated, and it was such a deliberate tease, it shouldn't have sent a long, dark spike of lust through his gut.

He pulled back a fraction, gratified when she swayed after him. "Rather do something else with me? All you have to do is ask."

Her irises flared, and he fell into the chocolaty depths. The expanse between them was an ocean, an eternity, the length of the universe, and he wanted to close the gap in the worst way. Holding back hurt. Badly. But he wanted to see if she'd take the plunge.

"Dax," she murmured and her breath fanned his face as she slid both hands on either side of his jaw. "There is something I want to do with you. Something I've been thinking about for a long time."

Whatever it was, he'd do it. This not-quite-a-kiss had him so thoroughly hot it was a wonder he didn't spontaneously combust. "What's that, sweetheart?"

"I want to beat you at your own game," she whispered and the gap vanished.

Hungrily, she devoured him, tongue slick against his, claiming it masterfully. Her hands guided his head to angle against her mouth more deeply, and fire shot through his groin, nearly triggering a premature release the likes of which he'd not had to fight back in almost two decades.

Groaning, he tried to gain some control, but she

eased him backward, hands gliding along his chest like poetry, fingers working beneath the hem to feel him up, and he couldn't stand it.

"Elise," he growled as she nipped at his ear. At the same moment, her fingernails scraped down his abs. White-hot lust zigzagged through the southern hemisphere.

They were in public. On purpose—to prevent anything too out-of-control from happening. Of course Elise had smashed that idea to smithereens.

He firmed his mouth and slowed it down. Way down. Languorously, he tasted her as he would fine wine and she softened under his kiss.

Emboldened now that he had the upper hand, he palmed the small of her back and hefted her torso against his. She moaned and angled her head to suck him in deeper, and he nearly lost his balance. Shifting to the back of the bench, he gripped her tighter, losing himself in the wave of sensations until he hardly knew which way was up.

They either needed to stop right now or take this behind closed doors. He pulled back reluctantly with a butterfly caress of his mouth against her temple.

It had to be the former. It was the middle of the day; he had to get back to work and see about the mess he'd left behind. She probably needed time to assess. Analyze. Work through her checklists and talk herself off the ledge.

Breathing hard, she pursed kiss-stung lips and peered at him under seductively lowered lashes. "Did I win?"

Eight

They held hands as they strolled back to Elise's office and she reveled in every moment of it. Dax didn't pause by his car, clearly intending to walk her all the way back inside. Maybe he was caught up in the rush and reluctant to part ways, too.

Wouldn't that be something? Dax Wakefield affected by Elise Arundel.

What was she *doing* with him?

For once, she had no idea and furthermore, didn't care. Or at least she didn't right now. Dax had a magic mouth, capable of altering her brain activity.

"Don't make plans for tonight," Dax said as they mounted the steps to her office. "I'll bring dinner to your house and we'll stay in."

That worked, and she refused to worry about lingering questions such as whether he intended to seduce her after dinner or if it would be a hands-off night. Maybe she'd seduce him before dinner instead.

She grinned, unable to keep the bubble of sheer bliss inside. This was her turn, her opportunity to get the guy.

"A date that's really a date because we're dating now?" she asked.

Insisting she still had to find him a different match had been an excuse, one contrived to avoid wanting him for herself—and to deny that the whole idea scared her. It still did. But it was her turn to be happy and hopefully make Dax happy at the same time. What could it hurt to try?

He scowled without any real heat. "Dating sounds like a label."

"I'm biting my tongue as we speak."

Unfortunately, she suspected she'd be doing a lot of that in the coming weeks. Somehow Dax had made it seem possible to forgo not only labels, but also guarantees about the future. But that didn't mean her personality had changed. She still wanted a happily ever after. She still wanted Dax to find true love.

The park-bench confessional had revealed more than either of them intended, of that she was sure. It was the only thing she was sure of. But she desperately wanted to believe that the raw revelations had opened them both up to trying something new in a relationship. Sticking around for Dax and day-by-day for her.

It required an extreme level of trust she wasn't sure she had in her. Day-by-day might be a blessing in disguise—it gave her time to figure out if she could trust Dax without wholly committing her fragile heart.

Dax opened the door to EA International and uttered an extremely profane word. She followed his gaze to see four women crowded around Angie's reception desk, all of whom turned in unison at the sound of the door. He dropped her hand without comment.

The park-bench kiss euphoria drained when she recognized Candy. The other three women, a brunette, a blonde and a redhead, weren't familiar but they all had a similar look about them as if they shared a hair stylist. And, like Candy, they all could have stepped from the pages of a magazine.

New clients referred by Candy? That seemed unlikely considering things hadn't worked out with

Dax. And Elise had yet to find Candy's soul mate. Guiltily, she made a mental note to go through Candy's profile again to see if she could fix that.

"Is this an ambush?" Dax asked and she did a double take at his granite expression.

"An ambush?" Elise repeated with a half laugh.

That was no way to speak to potential customers. She skirted him and approached the women with a smile. "I'm Elise Arundel. Can I help you?"

"We're here to protest." The redhead stepped to the front and gestured to the other ladies to show she spoke for the group. Not only did these women have similar styles, they also wore identical glowers.

Elise took a tiny step backward in her boots and wished she'd bought the Gucci ones with the higher heel.

"Protest?" Automatically, she shook her head because the word had no context. "I don't understand."

Angie shot to her feet, straightening her wool skirt several times with nervous fingers. "I'm sorry, Elise. I was about to ask them to leave."

Dax took Elise's elbow, his fingers firm against the sleeve of his jacket, and nodded to the redhead. "Elise, this is Jenna Crisp, a former girlfriend. You know Candy. Angelica Moreau is the one on the left and Sherilyn McCarthy is on the right. Also former girlfriends."

These were some of Dax's ex-girlfriends. She couldn't help but study the women with a more critical eye. It seemed Dax had been totally honest when he claimed to have no preference when it came to a woman's physical attributes. The women, though all beautiful and poised and polished, were as different as night and day.

Hard evidence of how truthfully Dax had answered at least one of the profile questions led her to wonder if he'd been forthright on all of them from the very beginning.

Which meant he really did think love was pure fiction.

A funny little flutter beat through Elise's stomach. Dax's hand on her arm was meant to comfort her—or hold her back—and she honestly didn't know which one she needed. "What exactly are you here to protest?"

Had Dax texted them with the news that he was interested in Elise or posted it to his Facebook timeline? He'd have to be very slick to have done so without Elise noticing and besides, why would he? None of this made any sense. It might be upsetting for a former girlfriend to find out Dax had moved on, but surely not surprising—the man was still underwear-model worthy, even fifteen years later, and could give Casanova *and* Don Juan kissing lessons.

Jenna crossed her arms and addressed Elise without glancing at Dax. "We're here in the best interest of your female clients. We're protesting you taking him on as a potential match. Don't foist him off on another unsuspecting woman."

Unable to stop blinking, Elise gaped at Jenna, extremely aware of the other women's hardened gazes. Those lined and mascaraed eyes might as well be spotlights.

"I'm sorry, what?"

A hot flush swept up from her neck to spread across her cheekbones. All those eyes on her, including Dax's and Angie's, had done their job to make her uncomfortable. After all, she was wearing Dax's huge jacket, which told its own story, but also turned her figure blocky, like a stout oak tree in a forest of willows.

"He's not interested in a relationship." Candy cleared her throat. "He told me. Flat out. I thought it was so strange. Why would he go to a matchmaker? Then Jenna and I met by accident at Turtle

Creek Salon and I found out he's only in your system as part of some wager the two of you made."

The other ladies nodded and the brunette said, "That's where we met Jenna and Candy too, at the salon."

They *did* share a hairdresser. Elise would congratulate herself on the good eye if it made one bit of difference. Her knees shook and she locked them.

Jenna waved at Dax. "He's a cold, heartless SOB who'll screw you over without a scrap of remorse. No woman deserves that in a match. You have to drop him as a client."

Dax's jacket gained about fifty pounds, weighing heavily on her shoulders. These women had no idea Elise had been kissing Dax not ten minutes ago and making plans to have dinner. But Jenna wasn't talking to her directly. Dax wasn't going to screw Elise over.

"This has gone on long enough." Dax stepped in front of Elise to position himself between her and the ex-girlfriends. "Say anything you like about me, but don't involve Elise in your grievances. She has a right to take on whomever she pleases as a client and you have no call to be here."

Dax's staunch defense hit her in the heart and

spread. He was a gentleman underneath his gorgeous exterior, and she appreciated the inside *and* the outside equally.

This was a really bad time to discover she might care about him more than she'd realized.

Jenna glared at Dax, fairly vibrating with animosity. "We were still together when you agreed to be a client. Did you tell her that? One would assume your matchmaker might like to know you weren't actually single."

The bottom dropped out of Elise's stomach. Surely that wasn't true. Jenna was spewing half truths in retaliation for Dax's imagined transgressions. That's what all of this was about—scorned women spewing their fury.

The blonde—Sherilyn, if Elise's beleaguered brain recalled correctly—flipped her curls behind her back and put a well-manicured comforting hand on Jenna's shoulder.

"We were dating, yes." Dax's eyes glittered. "But I was very much single. I did not promise you anything beyond our last date. If you chose to read a commitment into it, that's unfortunate, but it has nothing to do with my business at EA International. Nothing to do with Elise. You're using her to exact revenge on me and it won't work."

Let's take things day by day.

It was almost the same as saying no promises past the last date. Elise suspected Dax gave that speech often.

No, Dax was definitely not a liar. He was a player, exactly as advertised. None of these women had been able to change that and Elise couldn't either, whether she took it day by day or not. Her burden was deciding if she could live with no promises and the likelihood he'd be giving that speech to another woman in a few weeks, after he'd moved on from Elise.

Her fragile heart was already closer to the edge of that cliff on Heartbreak Ridge than she'd like.

All the eyes were back on her, burning into her skin. Jenna's were the hottest as she swept Elise with a pointed look that clearly indicated she found her lacking.

"It has everything to do with what kind of company this is. Are you a matchmaker or a gambler? Do women like Candy come in here expecting to meet a compatible man who's also looking for love, only to be disappointed and out a substantial sum of money?"

It was the TV interview all over again, except this time she wasn't naive enough to offer her matchmaking services to Jenna as a way to prove her skills. She had a hunch that woman ate men alive and then let them beg for more. Except for Dax. He'd truly hurt her.

Elise shook her head, hardly sure where to start slashing and burning Jenna's incorrect and provoking statements.

"I'm a matchmaker. Only. I care about helping people find love, even someone like Dax."

"Someone like Dax?" he repeated silkily as he focused his attention on Elise instead of Jenna. "What's that supposed to mean?"

And now everyone had turned against her, even the one person who'd been on her side. Who *should* have been on her side. She and Dax were embarking on something with no label, but which she'd wanted to explore. Or she had before she walked into this confrontation, this *ambush*.

The room started closing in. "It means you don't believe in love, and I naively thought I could show you how wrong you are. But I can't."

Her heart hurt to admit failure. Not only had she failed to accomplish a reversal in Dax's stance with a soul-mate match, she had almost set herself up for a more spectacular disaster by giving in to his day-by-day seduction routine.

She met the gaze of each ex-girlfriend in succession. It wasn't their fault they weren't the one and she held no hostility toward them.

"Dax is no longer a client as of today. So your protest is poorly timed. Candy, I'll refund your money. Expect the credit to appear on your statement within two days. Please see yourselves out."

She fled to her office and shut the door with an unsatisfying click. Slamming it would have been unprofessional and wouldn't have made her feel any less embarrassed. But it might have covered the sob in her throat.

The door immediately opened and Dax ended up on her side of it. He leaned against the closed door. "I'm sorry. I had no idea they were waiting around to pounce on you. It was uncalled for and entirely my fault."

She let her head drop into her hands so she didn't have to look at him. "It's not your fault. And I was talking to you, too, when I said see yourself out."

"I wanted to make sure you were okay."

The evident concern in his voice softened her. And it pissed her off that he could do that.

"I'm not. And you're the last person who can fix it."

"Elise." His hand on her shoulder shouldn't have

felt so right, so warm and like the exact thing she needed. "I have to get back to the office, but I'll make it up to you tonight."

Why did he have to be so sweet and sexy and so hard to pin down?

She shrugged it off—the hand, the man, the disappointment. "I can't do this with you."

"Do what? Have dinner with me? We've eaten plenty of meals together and you never had any trouble chewing before."

That was the problem. He wanted it to be dinner with nothing meaningful attached. In a few weeks, she'd end up like Jenna.

"Dinner isn't just dinner and you know it. It's a start and we have different ideas about what we're starting."

"That's completely untrue. Dinner is about spending time together. Making each other feel good. Conversation."

"Sex," she said flatly.

"Of course. I like sex. What's wrong with that?"

"Because I want to get married! I want to be in love. Not right away, but some day, and I need the possibility of that. I need the man I'm with to want those things too," she shouted.

Shouting seemed to be the only way to get

through to him. This was not going to work and he kept coming up with reasons why she should feel differently, as though there was something wrong with her because she didn't want to get in line behind the ex-girlfriends.

He swiveled her chair around to face him. "Maybe I will want that. And maybe you want those things but you'll realize you don't want them with me, and you'll think that's okay. Neither of us knows for sure what's going to happen. Nobody does."

No, but she had a pretty good idea what would happen, and it didn't lead to happily ever after. "Did you imagine yourself marrying Jenna while you were dating her?"

He flinched. "Don't let a few disgruntled women spook you."

The flinch answered the question as well as if he'd flat out said *no*.

"I'm not." That might have been the genesis, but the gang of ex-girlfriends had only brought suppressed issues to the surface. "This was a problem yesterday and the day before that. I let a few hot kisses on a park bench turn my brain off."

"So that's it then. You're done here?"

She didn't want to be. God help her, she couldn't let him walk away forever.

"I have more fun with you than with anyone else I've ever spent time with. If we can't be lovers, what's wrong with continuing to be friends?"

He let his hands fall to his sides. "That's what you want?"

"No, Dax. It's not what I want. But it's what I can offer you." She met his slightly wounded gaze without flinching, though her insides hurt to be so harsh. But what choice did she have? "Go back to work and if you still want to hang out *as friends,* you know where to find me."

Friends.

The word stuck in Dax's craw and put him in a foul mood for the remainder of the day. Which dragged on until it surely had lasted at least thirty-nine hours.

What did Elise want, a frigging engagement ring before they could have a simple *dinner* together? He'd never had so much trouble getting a woman to go on a date, let alone getting her between the sheets. He must be slipping.

"Dax?"

"What?" he growled and sighed as his admin

scurried backward over the threshold of his office door. "I'm sorry. I'm distracted."

It wasn't just Elise. The Stiletto Brigade of Former Girlfriends had been brutal, digging barbs into him with military precision. He treated women well while dating them, with intricately planned evenings at expensive venues, gifting them with presents. A woman never left his bed unsatisfied. So why all the animosity?

"You don't have to tell me. I needed those purchase orders approved by five o'clock." Patricia pointed at her watch. "Past five o'clock."

"Why can't Roy sign them? He's the CFO," he grumbled and logged in to the purchase order system so he could affix his digital approval to the documents. Why have a chief financial officer if the man couldn't sign a couple of purchase orders?

"Because they're over five hundred thousand dollars and Roy doesn't have that level of purchasing approval. Only the CEO does. As you know, since you put the policy in place," she reminded him with raised eyebrows. "Are you okay?"

"Fine."

He *was* fine. Why wouldn't he be fine? It wasn't as if he'd lost anything with Elise. They hadn't even slept together yet. A couple of really amazing kisses weren't worth getting worked up over.

Actually, to be precise, he and Elise had shared a couple of amazing kisses and a few good conversations. More than a few. Several.

"Why don't you go home?" Patricia asked.

To his lonely, industrial-size loft? Sure, that would fix everything. "Thanks, I will in a few minutes. You're welcome to leave. You don't have to wait on me."

She nodded, backing away from him as if she expected a surprise attack any second, and finally disappeared.

Dax messed around until well after six o'clock, accomplishing exactly zero in the process, and tried not to think about the Vietnamese place where he'd intended to pick up dinner before going to Elise's house. Vietnamese food warmed up well and he'd fully expected to let it get good and cold before eating.

So Elise hadn't been on board with taking their whatever-it-was-with-no-label to the next level after the run-in with the Stiletto Brigade. They'd freaked her out, right when he'd gotten her panic spooled up and put away.

Fine. He was fine with it.

Elise wanted all her check boxes checked before she'd commit to dinner. It was crazy. She'd rather be alone than spend a little time with a man who thought she was funny and amazing and wanted to get her naked.

Actually, that wasn't true. She was perfectly fine with being friends. As long as he kept his hands to himself and didn't complain when she made astute, painful observations about his relationship track record.

He fumed about it as he got into his car and gunned the engine. He fumed about it some more as he drove aimlessly around Dallas, his destination unclear.

Dax shook his off morose mood and focused on his surroundings. The side-street names were vaguely familiar but he couldn't place the neighborhood. He drove to the next stoplight, saw the name of the intersection, and suddenly it hit him.

He was a block from Leo's house.

House, fortress, same thing when it came to his former friend. Leo had excelled at keeping the world out, excelled at keeping his focus where it belonged—on success. Dax slowed as the car rolled toward the winding, gated drive. The huge manor skulked behind a forest of oaks, bits of light beaming between the branches stripped of leaves by the fall wind.

Was Leo at home? Hard to tell; the house was too far from the street. Once upon a time, Dax would have put money on the answer being no. For as long as he'd known Leo, the man worked until he nearly dropped with exhaustion. Occasionally, when Dax found himself between women, he'd coax his friend out from behind his desk and they'd tie one on at a bar in Uptown.

Case in point—Dax had no woman on call. No plans. It would have been a great night to meet up with a friend who didn't ask him pointed questions about why he never stuck it out with a woman longer than a few weeks.

He didn't call Leo. He didn't drive up to the security camera at the gate, which was equipped with facial recognition software, and would admit him instantly.

Leo wasn't that friend, not any more. Leo had a new playmate locked away inside his fortress, one he'd paid a hefty chunk of change to meet.

Well, not really a playmate since he'd married Daniella. *Married.* That was a whole lot of forever with the same woman. If Elise could be believed, Leo and Daniella were soul mates.

For the first time, Dax wondered if Leo was happy. Because wasn't that the point of a soul mate? You had someone you wanted to be locked away with, someone you could be with all the time and never care if the world spun on without either of you.

If Dax's soul mate existed, she would care very much what was behind his curtain and furthermore, he'd trust her with the backstage mess—the doubts about whether he actually had something to offer a woman in a relationship. The anxiety over whether he'd find out he had more in common with his mother than he'd like. The fear that he actually lacked the capacity to be with one person for the rest of his life. The suspicion that he was broken and that was why he'd never found someone worthy of promising forever to.

Five hundred thousand dollars seemed like a bargain if it bought a woman who stilled his restlessness. Dax had just spent twice that with the click of a mouse, and barely glanced at the description of the goods Wakefield Media had purchased. Whatever it was—likely cameras or other studio equipment—would either wear out or be replaced with better technology in a few years.

A soul mate was forever. How could that be possible for someone like Dax? What if he'd already met her and didn't realize it? That was the very definition of being broken, and it was exactly what Elise had meant when she'd said "someone like Dax."

Before he did something foolish, such as drive up to Leo's house and demand an explanation for how Leo had known Daniella was his soul mate, Dax hit the gas and drove until the low fuel light blinked on in the dash. He filled up the tank and went home, where he did not sleep well and his mood did not improve.

The next day dragged even worse than the day before. Everyone, including Patricia, steered clear, and while he appreciated their wisdom, it only pissed him off. He needed a big-time distraction.

Because he was in that perverse of a mood, he pulled out his phone and texted Elise.

Have a nice evening by yourself?

Well, that was stupid. Either she'd ignore him, tell him what a fabulous evening she had without him or make a joke that gave him zero information about whether she was in as bad of a mood as he was. And he wanted her to be. He wanted her to suffer for...

Beep. No. It sucked. I miss you.

His heart gave a funny lurch and the phone slipped from his nerveless fingers. God, what was he supposed to do with that?

Nothing. She was trying to manipulate him. She knew he didn't like to be alone and wanted him to crack first. That wasn't happening. He wasn't texting her back with some cheesy message about how he was miserable too. She was probably sitting there on that champagne-colored couch in her condo, phone in hand, waiting for his reply.

They weren't dating. Elise wasn't his lover. It shouldn't be this difficult.

He set the phone off to the side of his desk and proceeded to ignore it for the next thirteen minutes while he read the same paragraph of a marketing proposal over and over again.

The phone sat there, silently condemning him.

"Stop looking at me," he growled at the offending device and turned it over.

Elise wanted him to be some fairy-tale guy who swept her off her feet with promises of undying love, and it was so far from who he was, he couldn't even fathom it. So that was it. Nothing more to say or do.

The phone rang.

Elise. Of course she wasn't going to put up with

his stupid text embargo. His heart did that funny dance again as he flipped the phone over to hit the answer button.

"Hey, Dax," a female voice purred in his ear. It was not Elise.

Dang it. He should have at least glanced at the caller ID. "Hey…you."

He winced. He had no idea who she was.

"I've been thinking a lot about you since yesterday," she said.

Sherilyn. He recognized her voice now and if he hadn't been moping around like a lovesick teenager with an atrophied brain, he'd never have answered her call. "Yesterday when you and the rest of your wrecking crew stormed into a place of business and started telling the proprietor how to run it?"

Which wasn't too far off from what he'd done to Elise, but he'd staged his showdown over EA International's formula for success on TV. He swallowed and it went down his throat like razor blades. In his defense, at the time he hadn't known how much she hated being in the spotlight. She'd handled herself admirably, then and yesterday. Because she was amazing.

"Oh, I wasn't really a part of that." Sherilyn *tsk*ed. "I went along because I had a vested interest in seeing that you no longer had a shot at getting matched. I'm in the mood for round two with you."

What a mercenary.

"I'm sorry, Sherilyn, but I'm not interested in a relationship with anyone right now. You heard Candy. It would be unfair to you."

He did not want to have this conversation. Not with Sherilyn, not with Candy, not with any woman. He was sick of the merry-go-round.

"Come on. Remember how good it was?" Sherilyn laughed throatily. "I'm not asking for a commitment, Dax. Just one night."

Her words reverberated in his head, but he heard them in his voice, as he said them to Elise. And of course the idea had seemed as repugnant to Elise when it came from him as it did now to Dax coming from Sherilyn.

Why hadn't Elise slapped him? Instead, she'd offered him friendship, which he'd thrown back in her face because he'd wanted things his way, not hers. And he'd lost something valuable in the process.

Dax sighed. "No, actually, I don't remember. Thanks for calling, but please forget about me. We're not going to happen again."

He hung up and stared out the window of his office. He might as well go ahead and admit he missed Elise, too, and had no idea how to fix it.

The Stiletto Brigade hadn't caused his problem with her. The problem had been there from the beginning, as she'd said. He'd discounted Elise's hopes and dreams because they were based on something he considered absurd and improbable— true love. Yeah, he'd done the profile and gone along, but only to win the wager fairly, not because he believed she had some special ability to prove something that was impossible to prove. Yet she'd built an entire business on the concept, and if someone as smart as Leo bought into Daniella being his soul mate, maybe there was more to the idea than Dax had credited.

Maybe he should give Elise's way a chance.

Or...

Love was a myth and now that some time had passed, the new marriage smell had worn off, but Leo was too embarrassed to admit he'd made a mistake. If Dax gave in to Elise without more information, he could be setting himself up for a world of hurt. After all, he didn't trust easily for a reason. Look what had happened to his friendship with Leo.

Besides, Elise wanted to meet her soul mate and Dax was not it. Their vastly different approaches to relationships—and to life as a whole—proved that. So why pretend?

There was nothing wrong with two consenting adults having fun together. They didn't have to swear undying devotion to take their relationship to the next level.

Why was she being so *stubborn* about this?

Leo might be too ashamed to come clean about how disastrous his relationship had become with Daniella, but Elise had lots of other clients. Surely several of EA International's former matches hadn't lasted. An unhappily ever after was a better way to attest that love was a myth than being matched with another Candy, anyway.

All he needed was one couple who hadn't ended up with their soul mate as advertised. Then he could take the evidence to Elise. She needed to understand how the real world worked, and what better way to convince her? He'd have hard proof that even when people started out wanting a lifelong commitment, sometimes it still didn't happen. Sure, she might be a little upset at first to learn she'd held out for something that didn't exist, but then she'd see his point. She wanted him as much

as he wanted her, and it was time to let things between them take their natural course.

Guarantees were for products, not people. By
this time tomorrow, he could have Elise naked and
moaning under his mouth.

Nine

Saturday night, Elise finally stopped carrying her phone around in her hand. Dax hadn't called, hadn't texted, hadn't dropped by. He wasn't going to. The line had been drawn, and instead of doing something uncomfortable like stepping over it, Dax had hightailed it in the other direction. His loss.

And hers, unfortunately. She couldn't shake a slight sense of despondency, as though she hadn't seen the sun in weeks and the forecast called for more rain.

It was a good thing she'd put on the brakes when she had—imagine how hurt she'd be if things had gone any further. Regardless, she was undeniably disappointed he didn't even want to stay friends, which she had to get over.

She needed to focus on Blanca and Carrie, the two new applicants in her makeover program. They were both due to arrive in a couple of weeks and Elise had done almost nothing to prepare.

She tapped out a quick email to Dannie, who helped Elise with makeup and hair lessons when needed. After years at the knee of a supermodel, Elise had enough fashion and cosmetic tips to fill an ocean liner, but Dannie liked the work and by now, the two women were fast friends.

Elise confirmed the dates and attached a copy of a contract for Dannie's temporary employment. Normally, it wouldn't be a question of whether Dannie would say yes, but she and Leo had just returned from an extended vacation to Bora Bora in hopes Dannie would come home pregnant.

Elise would be thrilled if that was the reason Dannie said no.

Then she made a grocery list as two extra mouths required a great deal of planning, especially to ensure the meals were healthy but not too difficult to prepare. Few of the women in her program came to her with great culinary skills. It was one of the many aspects of training she offered, and after a lifelong love-hate relationship with food, Elise brought plenty to the literal and figurative table.

The remainder of the evening stretched ahead of her, long and lonely. She flipped on a movie, but her mind wandered.

The doorbell startled her and she glanced at the clock. Good grief, it was nearly midnight. It could only be Dax. A peek through the window confirmed it. Despite the shadows, she'd recognize the broad set of his shoulders and lean figure anywhere.

Her heart lightened. She'd missed him, fiercely.

She took a half second to fortify herself. He could be here for any number of reasons. Better to find out straight from the horse's mouth than get her hopes up.

"I wasn't expecting you," she said needlessly as she opened the door and cursed the jumpy ripples in her stomach. He was just so masculine and gorgeous. Then she got a good look at his face. The sheer darkness in his gaze tore through her. "What's wrong?"

Tension vibrated through the air as he contemplated her. "I don't know why I'm here."

"Bored? Lonely? Can't find anyone else who wants to play?" She crossed her arms over her middle. Something was up and it was far more chilling than the frigid fall night.

"On the contrary," he said smoothly, his voice like pure honey. "Women seem to be coming out of the woodwork. Except for the one I really want."

Her?

Why was that so affecting in places better left unaffected? It should irritate her to be thought of as an object of lust. The idea shouldn't feel so powerful and raw. But a week's worth of being on edge and missing their verbal swordplay and dreaming about his abs culminated in a heated hum in her core.

"I..." *Want you too.* "...hoped you'd call."

"Did you?" He hooked his thumbs in the front pockets of his jeans, but the lethal glint in his eye belied the casual pose. "What did you hope I'd say? Let's be friends? Let's paint each other's nails and shop for shoes together?"

She should shut the door. She should tell him to go away and forget she'd ever mentioned being friends.

"I hoped you'd unbend enough to admit there's a possibility you might fall in love one day. Barring that, I hoped you'd still want to have lunch occasionally or—"

"Elise. I don't want to be your friend."

"Not worth it to you?" she snapped.

"It's not enough." His hands fisted against his pockets and she realized he was trying to keep himself under control. "I wasn't going to call. I wasn't going to come over. I found myself within a block of your house five times this week all the same."

"But you kept driving."

He nodded once. "I kept driving. Until tonight."

After a long pause, she voiced the question he obviously wanted her to ask. "What was special about tonight?"

"I can't—I don't know how to give you what you want," he bit out. "And I don't know how to stay away."

Her heart stuttered and shoved all her suppressed feelings to the surface. That's why she'd missed him—when he showed her glimpses of his soul, it was more beautiful than the ocean at sunset.

"I never asked you to stay away. You shouldn't have."

"Yes. I should have. I absolutely should not be here on your doorstep." His chest shuddered with his next deep breath. "But I can't sleep. I can't concentrate. All I can think about is you naked, wrapped around me, and that brain of yours firing away on all cylinders as you come up with more inventive ways to challenge me."

The image of her unclothed body twined with his sprang into her consciousness, sparked through her abdomen, raised goose bumps on her skin. She swallowed against the sudden burn in her throat.

"You say that like it's a bad thing," she joked and nearly bit her tongue as fire licked through his expression.

"It's ridiculous. And I'm furious about it, so stop being so smug."

His glare could have melted ice. All at once, his strange mood made sense. Normally when he wanted a woman, he seduced all her reservations away. But he respected Elise too much to do that to her and he was incredibly conflicted about it. The effect of that realization was as powerful as being the object of his desire.

Combined, it nearly took her breath.

"Poor thing," she crooned. "Did that bad Elise tie you up in knots?"

One brow lifted and every trace of his ire disappeared, exactly as she'd intended. "Don't you dare make a suggestion like that unless you plan to follow through."

"Uh-uh." She shook her head. "This conversation is not devolving into foreplay."

"Not yet." Lazily, he swept her with a half-lidded smoky once-over. "But I appreciate the confirmation that talking dirty to you counts as foreplay."

Now she should slam the door in his cocky face. Except she'd shifted the mood on purpose, to give him a reprieve for confessing more than he'd probably intended. And the last thing she wanted was for him to leave.

But did she want him to stay? This wasn't some random drive-by; it was a showdown.

Between his mercurial mood and the hum in her core, this night could end up only one of two ways—either she'd let him into her bed and into her heart, or she'd give him that final push away.

Dax was still on the porch. Waiting for her to make the decision. And Dax would never let her forget she'd made the choice.

Who was tying whom up in knots here?

"Why are you here, Dax?" She took a tiny step behind the door, in case she needed to slam it after all. Of course there was a good chance he'd slam it for her, once he crossed the threshold and backed her up against it in a tango too urgent and wild to make it past the foyer. "And don't feed me another line. You know exactly why you got out of the car this time."

His reckless smile put her back on edge. "Why do I find it so flipping sexy when you call me on my crap?"

He thought her no-filter personality was sexy. He really did. She could see the truth of it in his expression. The wager was over and there was no reason for him to say something like that unless he meant it.

"Because you're neurotic and deranged, obviously." When his smile softened, she couldn't help but return it, along with a shrug. "We both must be. If you want the real answer, you said it yourself. You like that I challenge you. If it's easy, you don't value it as much."

His irises flashed, reflecting the bright porch light. "I would definitely classify this as not easy."

"And you still haven't told me why you're here."

He crossed his arms and leaned on the door frame. "Have you ever followed up with any of the couples you've matched?"

"Of course. I use them as referrals and I throw parties every few months for both former and current clients as a thank-you for being customers. Many become friends."

"They're all happy. All of them. They've all

found their soul mates and say you were one hundred percent responsible." He said it as if Elise had single-handedly wiped out a small village in Africa with a virus.

"You talked to my former clients?"

The shock wasn't that he'd done so, but that he'd *just* done so. Why hadn't he had those conversations at the very beginning, when they were still operating under the terms of the wager?

"Not the recent ones, only those matched over five years ago. They should be miserable by now. Happily ever after doesn't exist." His rock-hard expression dared her to argue with his perfunctory statement.

Except he'd learned otherwise, and clearly it was throwing him for a loop.

He hadn't talked to her clients before now because he'd assumed he didn't need to. That he'd only be told what he already believed to be true.

It was hard to be handed back your arrogance on a silver platter.

"I offer a guarantee, Dax," she reminded him gently. "No one's ever asked for their money back."

Instead of bowing and scraping with apology, he stared at her. "Aren't you going to invite me in?"

"Why would I do that?"

His gaze burned through her. "Because you want to know what else I learned when I talked to your clients."

He'd learned *more* than happily ever after happened to people on a regular basis? Oh, yes, he had and he was going to make her work to find out what, running her through his maze until she dropped with exhaustion. Or solved it and won the prize. It was a ludicrous challenge. And it was working.

But she didn't for a moment believe he only wanted to tell her about his findings. The prize wasn't simply information and they both knew it.

She held the door open wide in silent invitation and prayed she wasn't going to be sorry.

She shouldn't have answered the bell. But now she had to know if talking to happy couples had somehow opened his eyes. Maybe gotten him to a place where he could see a future with one woman.

What if she *could* be that woman? She didn't want to send him on his way before finding out.

"Dax?"

He met her gaze as he stepped over the threshold. "Elise."

Searching his beautiful face for some small scrap of reassurance, she put it all on the line.

"Please don't do this unless you mean it."

* * *

Dax shut the door behind him and leaned back against it, both hands flat against the wood.

The click reverberated in the silent foyer.

Elise's eyes were shiny and huge and he didn't mistake the look for anything other than vulnerability, which just about did him in where the last week of awfulness hadn't.

Why had he stayed away so long?

It didn't matter now. He was surrounded by Elise and everything finally made sense again. He breathed her in before he hauled her into his arms right there in the foyer.

Tonight wasn't about slaking his thirst in the well of Elise, though he'd be lying if he said he wasn't hopeful they'd eventually get there. He'd have sworn this was all about taking pleasure where pleasure was due. But now that he was here…it wasn't. He still wasn't sure *what* tonight was about, what he truly wanted—or what she wanted—but the fragile quality to her demeanor wasn't doing his own brittle psyche any favors.

Don't do this unless you mean it.

He didn't pretend to misunderstand. Her voice broke as she'd said it and it echoed in his head, demanding an answer—which he didn't have.

They needed to shake off the heaviness.

"Don't do what?" he asked lightly. "Tell you about the nineteen conversations I had with blissfully happy couples? It was nauseating."

Her quick smile set off an explosion of warmth in his midsection.

"Nineteen? That's a lot of conversations about true love. What I don't get is why you'd subject yourself to that."

He shrugged. "Seek-and-destroy mission. I was sure I'd find at least one couple embroiled in a bitter divorce settlement. Needless to say, no one was. On the heels of that estrogen ambush in your office, I needed to figure out some things."

Guilt flickered across Elise's face. "I'm sorry that happened. Some of that must have been really hard to stomach, especially coming from women you were formerly intimate with. I was selfishly caught up in my own reaction and didn't think about how you must have felt."

"Uh…" He'd been about to brush it away. But this was Elise. She'd see through him in a second. How had she known the whole thing had bothered him so much?

So much for lightening the mood.

"I was more worried about you than me," he said gruffly. "But thanks."

Such a small word to encompass the full generosity of Elise's apology. A lot of women—most women—would have said he'd gotten what was coming to him. And maybe he had. He'd treated Jenna pretty shabbily. He sighed. There was a possibility all of the women had genuine grievances. Relationships were not his forte.

But he wanted that to be different.

Elise motioned him out of the foyer and walked into the living room. "So while talking with my clients, what did you figure out?"

He followed, caught up with her in a couple of steps and grasped her hand to swing her around to face him in front of a gas-log fireplace, the flame lowered to a romantic glow.

Don't do this unless you mean it.

But that was exactly it. He *wanted* meaning, wanted something to finally click.

"I figured out *I'm* the one missing something." And only Elise held the answer. "I got out of the car tonight because I want to know what it is. You're the relationship expert. Tell me."

Her skin was luminous in the firelight and he wanted to trace the line of her throat with his lips, then keep going to discover the delights of the trim body waiting for him under her off-white sweater. But he wanted to hear her response just as much.

She looked up, hand still in his. Flesh to flesh, it sparked and the answering awareness leaped into her expression. Something powerful that was part chemistry and part something else passed between them. He let it, embraced it, refused to disrupt the moment simply because he'd been off balance since the moment this woman insisted he call her Ms. Arundel.

He tightened his grip. He wasn't about to let her step away, either.

"Tell me what I'm missing, Elise."

"What if I show you?" Her voice scraped at him, raw and low.

"What if you did?" he murmured. "What does that look like?"

"It looks like two people connecting on a fundamental level." Without breaking eye contact, she slid her free hand up his chest and let it rest over his heart, which sped up under her fingers. "It looks like the start of a long kiss that you can't bear to end. It looks like a friendship that's made more beautiful because you've opened your soul along with your body. Have you ever had that before?"

"No," he said, shocked at the catch in his throat. Shocked at how much he suddenly wanted something he'd had no clue existed.

"Me, either."

The wistful note of her admission settled over him heavily, binding them together in mutual desire for something meaningful and special.

"How do we get it?"

"It's right here," she whispered, tapping the place over his heart once with an index finger, then touching her own heart. "For both of us. All we have to do is reach out at the same time. That's what makes it wonderful."

Everything inside woke up at once, begging to dive into not just the sensations, but the swirl of the intangible. He'd called off the wager strictly because he'd begun to suspect he was about to lose. Spectacularly. And as he looked into her soul, it was done.

He was lost.

"Elise." He palmed her chin and lifted those luscious lips to his and hovered above them in a promise of pleasures to come. "I mean it."

And then he fell into that long kiss he hoped would never end and wrapped Elise in his arms. When his knees buckled, he took her to the carpet with him, twisting to break her fall, sliding into a chasm of pure joy.

She found the hem of his shirt and spread her palms hot against his back. He groaned and angled his head to take the kiss deeper, to explore her with his tongue, to taste the beauty of her.

This wasn't an urgent coupling, a slaking of mutual thirst. It was more. Much more. Profound and meaningful. And he couldn't have stopped if his life depended on it.

He wanted Elise. Wanted it all, everything she'd offered, especially the emotional connection.

She lifted her head a fraction. "Dax?"

"Hmm?" He took the opportunity to run his lips down the column of her neck, exactly as he'd envisioned, and yes, it was sweet. She moaned, letting her head fall back to give him better access.

"Don't you want to go upstairs?" she asked after a good long minute of letting him taste her.

Upstairs was far away and required too much effort to get there.

"Not especially. I don't think I can wait that long." That gorgeous blush rose up in her cheeks. Mystified, he ran the pad of his thumb over the coloring. "What's this all about?"

"We're in the living room," she whispered.

"I know," he whispered back and snaked a hand under her sweater to feel the curve of her waist in an intense caress. "I'm becoming very fond of your living room. The fireplace is a nice touch."

"I just...you know. The living room is for watching TV. The bed is for...lying down. In the dark."

More blushing. Despite the rock-hard bulge in his pants and the near-breathless state of desire she'd thrown him into, he recognized a woman in the midst of uncertainty. But over what?

"I'm not a particular fan of darkness. I want to see you."

"There's uh...not much to see." She wiggled a little until his hand fell from her waist, and then she yanked the hem of her sweater down over her exposed skin with a little too much force.

Sitting back on the carpet a bit to give her space, he reached out and took her hand gently. The last thing he wanted was for her to be uncomfortable. "What happened to opening yourself body and soul? Isn't that what this is about?"

"Easier said than done." She made a face. "Especially when I'm up against such stiff competition."

Competition?

Then it dawned on him. The Stiletto Brigade. They'd not only spooked her, they'd given Elise a complex about her appearance. His heart flipped over painfully but when it faded, a strange sort of tenderness replaced it.

"Look at me." When she complied, the earlier vulnerability was back tenfold. "There's not a way to say this without sounding arrogant, but roll with it for a minute. Don't you think I could be in the bed of any woman I chose?"

Her brows furrowed. "Yeah, but that wasn't really in question."

He gave her a minute but her anxiety didn't fade. A smart woman was still susceptible to being deceived by her own self-consciousness, apparently. "Then wouldn't it be safe to assume I'm with the woman I want? And that I think you're beautiful beyond compare?"

Except he'd done almost nothing to convince her of that because their relationship had evolved in such an out-of-the-norm manner. He'd never sent her flowers, never bought her jewelry, and certainly never spent an evening flattering her over dinner.

But he didn't want to do those things with her. He'd done them with other women. A lot. And it had never amounted to more than a shallow bit of nothingness designed to get a woman in bed.

Elise deserved better.

He slid a hand through her hair and smoothed it away from her face. "Instead of telling you how I feel about you, how about if I show you?"

Ten

The corners of Elise's mouth lifted. "What does that look like?"

Obviously she'd recognized her own words as he repeated them back to her.

"It looks like something so stunning, I can hardly breathe." Watching her intently, he fingered the hem of her sweater and lifted it slowly until her stomach was bared. Then he stopped. "Do you trust me with the rest?"

Surprise flitted through her expression. "I…I never thought about this being about trust."

"Of course it is. We're reaching out at the same time, but doing so requires a measure of faith. On both sides."

She stilled, taking it all in, and in a flash, he got the distinct sense she had a lot less experience with men and sex in general than the majority of women he knew. She talked such a good game he'd missed it, but with all the discussion around competition and being embarrassed about the locale he'd chosen, not to mention how often he found her home alone on the weekends…it all fit.

Then she nodded and lifted her arms, silently offering him access to completely remove her top—and placing utter trust in him at the same time. It just about broke him. Sucking in oxygen, which did not settle his racing pulse, he took his time unveiling her, inch by creamy, gorgeous inch.

She wasn't wearing a bra. And her breasts were perfect, topped by peaks that went rigid under his heated gaze. He muttered a curse as his hands involuntarily balled up, aching to stroke her from neck to belly button. *Take it slow, Wakefield.*

"You're exquisite," he ground out through a throat gone frozen, and tossed the sweater aside, unable to tear his attention from her half-naked form. Nonsense spilled from his mouth, murmured words of praise and awe. So maybe he'd tell her how much he liked her body in addition to showing her.

"Your turn," she whispered.

Immediately he complied, whipping his shirt off as fast as humanly possible because there was no way he was letting fabric block his ability to drink in the sight of gorgeous, uncovered Elise.

"Look your fill," he advised her. "Here in the light."

Look her fill she did, hesitantly at first but then with a hungry boldness that somehow turned erotic instantly. As her gaze traveled over his bare torso, heat flushed across his skin and coalesced at the base of his spine. All the blood in his head rushed south, leaving him slightly dizzy and enormously turned on.

She was going to kill him.

"Get used to me without clothes," he continued. "I'm about to be a whole lot more naked. I want you to see how much you affect me when I look at you. How much I want you, how gorgeous you are to me."

No time like the present to shed his jeans. He stood and with the heat of the fire at his back and the heat of Elise at his front, he flipped the button. She watched, silently, her head tipped up and her lips parted, hands clasped in her lap tightly.

He should have opened with a striptease because she'd totally forgotten her own nakedness. Win-win.

Then he was fully undressed and she huffed out a strangled gasp. It was potent to render a woman with such a quick wit speechless.

"See this?" he pointed at the obvious erection straining toward her. "This is all you, honey. You're not even touching me and I'm about to bust."

He wasn't kidding. Show and Tell was turning into his favorite foreplay game ever.

"What if I wanted to touch you?" she asked coyly. "Is that allowed?"

He strangled over a gasp of his own. "That's more than allowed. In fact, it's encouraged."

Crawling to him, she wiggled out of the remainder of her clothes unprompted and knelt at his feet.

With incredible care, she ran her hands up his legs, fingering the muscles of his thighs, breezing by his erection. She grazed it and his eyelids fluttered with the answering spike of unadulterated pleasure.

She climbed to her feet to continue her exploration and he fought to stay still. Every nerve vibrated on full alert, poised to pounce at the first opportune moment.

"You still have gorgeous abs," she murmured

as her fingertips read the muscles of his torso like braille. "They feel like warm, velvet stone."

"Looked me up on Google, did you?" He grinned, pleased for some ridiculous reason. Millions of people had seen those ads and he'd never given it a moment's thought. But the idea of Elise taking secret pleasure in looking at pictures of him—it was hot. "Put your hands a little south of my abs and you'll find something else that feels like velvet stone."

There came the blush again and he should totally be chagrined that he'd provoked it on purpose. But he wasn't.

Glancing at the real estate in question and back up again quickly, she gave a little sigh of appreciation that sang right through him. "I do that to you? Really?"

He groaned in disbelief and frustration. "You have been for weeks and weeks. Years. For an eternity. And now I'm moving on to the 'show' part of this demonstration."

Catching her up in his arms, he fitted hungry lips to her mouth and let all the pent-up desire guide the kiss. Instantly, she melted against him and he took full advantage, winding his embrace tighter to fit her luscious little body against him.

She felt amazing, warm and soft, and he wanted to touch. So he did, running his hands down her back, along the sweet curve of her rear, and he nearly cried out when she responded in kind. Her hands were bold and a bit clumsy with eagerness and combined, it swirled into a vortex of need more powerful than any he'd ever felt before.

This was so far beyond simply taking pleasure and returning it, he couldn't fathom it.

The urge to make this cataclysmic for her became more important than breathing.

He picked her up easily and laid her out on the couch where he could focus on loving every inch of her. Kneeling between her amazing legs, he inched over her until they were skin to skin, but his full weight rested on his elbows on either side of her.

"Talk to me," he murmured as he nuzzled her neck.

"Talk to you about what?" she asked.

He lifted his head so he could speak to her directly.

"Tell me what you like, Elise."

As passionate as she was about connection and relationships, she'd probably be incredibly responsive to anything he did, but he'd prefer to start out educated.

She bit her lip, contemplating. "Shoes. And this is a horrible thing to admit, but I really, really like chocolate."

He couldn't even laugh. She truly had no clue he'd meant for her to tell him what she liked sexually. Probably no one had ever asked her before or she had less experience than he'd assumed. The seriousness of the trust she'd shown hit him in a place inside he'd never realized was there.

"Why is it horrible to like chocolate?"

"Because it goes straight to my hips. I gain weight easily."

"That's impossible." Because he wanted to and he could, he shifted onto his side and ran the back of his hand down the curve of her waist, over the not-chunky hip and around her thigh, and it was nice indeed. "You're so thin you'd have to run around in the shower to get wet."

She snorted. "Thanks, but I didn't always look like this."

The small slice of pizza, the unfinished lunches, came back to him suddenly. She really didn't eat much. And somehow, this fear of gaining weight was tied to her self-image issues.

"You'd be beautiful to me even if you weighed more." In fact, she could stand to gain a few pounds.

"I thought we were doing the show part," she said pertly and slid her leg along his, opening herself without seeming to realize it. It was so unconsciously sexy, he let her change the subject. Plus, the new subject was one he happened to approve of.

"Yeah?" he growled. "You like it when I show you how much you turn me on? Let's begin with exhibit A."

And then he mouthed his way down her stomach to the juncture of her thighs, parting them easily, and she gasped as he tasted her sweet spot, laving it lightly to give her time to adjust to such an intimate kiss.

Her hips rolled, shoving his lips deeper against her wet center, and he sucked. She moaned on a long note and that was it—she pulsed against his tongue with a little cry that he felt clear to his toes. His own release almost transpired right then and there. It took all he had to keep it together.

He couldn't wait to be inside her any longer.

Slipping on a condom with quick fingers, he rose up over her and caught her gaze, communicating without words, letting all his desire for her spill from his expression. She stared back, eyes luminous with satisfaction.

Slowly, so slowly, he bent one of her gorgeous legs up and nestled between her thighs to complete their connection. She sighed lustily as he pushed. When he'd entered her fully, a wash of pleasure slammed his eyelids shut and he groaned in harmony with her.

It was a dazzling thing to be joined with Elise, and he couldn't hold back. Her name tumbled from his lips, over and over, as he spiraled them both higher. Nearly mindless, he sought to touch her, to caress her, to make her come again before he did…because there were rules. But she shifted, and the angle was so sweet, he lost complete control. Splintering into oblivion, he cried out as answering ripples of her climax sharpened his. The powerful orgasm sucked him under for a long moment, blinding him to everything but the release.

With the fireplace crackling merrily and the warmth of an amazing afterglow engulfing him, he lay there, unable to move. Elise cradled his spent body, both of their chests heaving as one, and he experienced the most profound sense of bliss.

That's what he'd missed.

Happily ever after just might begin with one day of happiness that you found so amazing and wonderful, you woke up the next day aching to repeat it. And didn't let anything stop you.

Elise finally coaxed Dax into bed and they thoroughly christened it in what was the most monumentally earth-shattering experience of her admittedly short list of sexual encounters. So far, she'd managed to keep her total cluelessness from him, but she couldn't let this particular first slide.

She snuggled up against his absolutely delicious body and waited until he'd pulled the sheet up around them to spill it. "You're the first man I've had in this bed."

"Ever?" His voice was soft with a hint of wonderment. As if she'd given him a special gift he'd always wanted but never received.

Was she *that* far gone over a couple of orgasms? She was assigning all kinds of emotions to Dax that she had no business assigning. Her head needed to be plucked out of the clouds really fast, before she got ideas about what was going on here that would only lead to disappointment.

She'd consented to sleep with him, but not to fall for him.

She nodded against his shoulder and opted for candor. "I bought this set about a year ago and I didn't want to sleep here night after night with memories of a past relationship gone wrong still haunting it."

The hand intimately caressing her waist stilled. "Guess that means you figured out how to exorcise the ghosts of past lovers. Or you think I'll be in your bed for the rest of its life."

The post-orgasm high vanished as the heaviness of his real question weighted the atmosphere.

"Um…" Well, she really hadn't thought through how that particular confession was going to go, had she? "Door number three. I thought you were worth it regardless."

He slid a hand up to her jaw and guided her head up so he could look at her. Something misty and tender sprang from his gaze. "That's the best thing anyone's ever said to me."

How could that be? Surely someone had told him he had value before. But his expression said otherwise.

She couldn't look away as a powerful and intangible current arced between them. It was more than the connection she'd told him was possible.

More than the deepening of their friendship that she'd sought.

Then he laid his lips on hers in a sweet kiss that went on and on and sent her into the throes of a whole different kind of high. So what if her head was firmly in the clouds?

She was in bed with Dax and he was beautiful and precious and it was the most amazing night in her memory.

And it didn't appear to be ending anytime soon.

"Lay here with me." He spooned her against his warm torso and held her as if he'd never let go, as if it was the most natural thing in the world.

"So are you...staying?" She bit her lip and left it at that, though the question was so much bigger.

"What, you mean overnight?" he mumbled. "Since it's nearly two a.m., I assumed that was pretty much a given. Do you want me to leave?"

"No!" Horrified, she snuggled deeper into him in apology and his arms tightened. The last thing she wanted was to wake up alone. "Just checking. I'm happy with you where you are."

No man had ever slept in this bed, either, and she wasn't sorry she'd waited for Dax to be the first. He fit into it perfectly and if he wasn't careful, she would invite him to spend a good long while in it.

That was actually what she'd hoped to establish by asking whether he planned to stay. Not just overnight, but when tomorrow came, then what? Was it too soon to talk about it? Was it implied that this was the start of a relationship in every sense?

Or was she supposed to know this was one night only?

"Good. Get some sleep. You're going to need it. And Elise," he whispered in her ear. "I might stay tomorrow night, too."

Apparently he'd read her thoughts.

Whether she'd given herself permission or not, it was too late to pretend she wasn't falling for him. She tucked the feeling away and held it close to her heart.

She fell asleep with a smile on her face and woke up with the same smile. Dax made her happy and she wanted to do the same for him. But he wasn't in the bed. Covers thrown back, his side was already cool. Frowning, she strained to hear the shower. Nothing.

He wasn't downstairs either. She sighed and pulled the sash on her robe tighter, cursing herself for thinking…well, it didn't matter. Dax was free to leave. She'd just hoped he wouldn't. He hadn't made promises—false or otherwise—and she hadn't requested any.

But she'd put a lot of faith in him based on his insistence that he meant it and his pretty speech about trust. Perhaps she should have established a better understanding of his definition of "I mean it."

When the front door swung open and Dax called out cheerily, she nearly dropped her freshly brewed cup of coffee.

Dax sauntered into the kitchen all windblown and smiley. It shouldn't be possible to look that delicious after only a few hours of sleep. She didn't bother to hide her openmouthed gaping.

He dropped a kiss on her temple and handed her a bag. "Hey, gorgeous. Bagels. I hope that's okay. Breakfast is the most important meal of the day, after all." He grinned and eyed her robe. "But now I'm wondering what's underneath there. Breakfast can wait a few minutes, can't it?"

"Maybe. Depends on how good the bagels are." She smiled as he glared at her in mock dismay. Then she noticed the other bag, hanging from his shoulder. "That, um, looks like a suitcase. Taking a trip?"

He shrugged. "Picked up a few things while I

was out. I don't live far. Figured I'd like to be dressed in an actual suit Monday morning when I show up for work."

Oh, my. Obviously he'd decided to spend Sunday with her. And the whole of Sunday night too. Dare she hope he'd undergone such a miraculous conversion that he was ready to spend every waking second with her?

Or was this blissful weekend the beginning of the end?

"So what are we doing here?" she blurted out, suddenly panicked and quite unable to pinpoint why. "You're staying all day, tonight and then what? I'm sorry, I can't just go with it. I need some parameters here."

The bag dropped to the floor and he leaned against the kitchen counter, his expression blank. "What kind of parameters do you want? I thought this was a pretty good compromise, bringing some stuff over. It's not day by day, but no one's made any promises they can't keep. Were you expecting me to show up with more stuff?"

She'd been expecting *less* stuff, far less. She had no idea what to do with all the stuff he'd unloaded. Relationships were supposed to be structured, predictable. Weren't they? Why hadn't she practiced a

whole lot more before this one? The two relationships she'd been in before were vastly inadequate
preparation for Dax Wakefield.

"I wasn't actually expecting you to show up at
all," she confessed. "I thought you'd bailed."

"I sent you a text. Isn't that our thing?" He
grinned. "I thought you slept with your phone in
your hand, pining for a message from me. That
takes me down a few notches."

Frowning, she scouted about for her phone and
finally found it in the side pocket of her purse. On
silent. She thumbed up the message.

Don't eat. I'll be back asap with breakfast. Can't
wait to see you.

All righty then. She blew out a breath and it
turned into a long sigh. She kept looking for reasons not to trust him and he hadn't disappointed
her yet. What was her *problem?*

"Hey." He pulled her into his arms and rested his
head on top of hers. "You really thought I wasn't
coming back? You don't do one-night stands. I respect that. I wouldn't have come here last night if
I didn't."

"Sorry," she mumbled into his shirt in case she'd
offended him. In truth, he didn't sound anything
other than concerned but she'd somehow lost the

ability to read him. That scared her. "I'll shut up now."

"I don't want you to shut up." Pulling back slightly, he peered down at her. "Your mouth is the sexiest thing on you."

With that, the tension mostly blew over. Or rather she chose to ignore the lingering questions so she could enjoy spending the day with a man she liked, who liked her back. It *was* a good compromise—for now. She didn't like not knowing the plan or what to expect. But for today, she knew Dax would be in her bed at the end of it and that was something she readily looked forward to.

They had fun giggling together over a couple of Netflix movies and ate Chinese delivery for lunch.

"Let me take you someplace really great for dinner," he suggested as he collected the cartons to dispose of them. "If you'll actually eat, that is."

He hefted her half-full takeout carton in deliberate emphasis.

"I'm not all that hungry," she said out of habit, and then made the mistake of glancing up into his slightly narrowed gaze, which was evaluating her coolly. Of course he hadn't bought that excuse.

Instead of taking the trash to the kitchen as he should have, Dax set the cartons back on the coffee table and eased onto the cushion next to her. "Elise—"

"I ate most of it. There's no crime in not being hungry." Her defensive tone didn't do much for her case.

"No, there's not." He contemplated her for a few long moments. "Except you're never hungry. I didn't press you on it last night when you told me you gain weight easily because, well, I was a little busy, but I can't ignore it forever. Do you have a problem I should know about?"

"Like anorexia?" The half laugh slipped out before she could catch it. This was not funny *at all* but he'd caught her by surprise. "I like food far too much to starve myself entirely, thanks."

How had the conversation turned heavy so fast? And when precisely had they reached a point in their relationship where it was okay to throw it all out there, no censor, no taboos?

"Maybe not *entirely,*" he stressed. "But you don't like yourself enough to have a healthy relationship with food either."

Gently, he took her hand and she let him. His concern was evident. But he could stop with all the psychobabble any time now. She didn't have a problem other than an intense desire to never be fat again. Nothing wrong with that.

"Thanks for checking in, but it's okay. My health *is* my concern." She glanced away. He saw too much but it was the price for opening up to him. "This will be hard for you to sympathize with, I realize, but I was an ugly duckling for a long time. A fat girl. When I finally lost all the weight, I vowed never to gain it back. Portion control is my friend."

"Elise." He stroked her knuckles with his thumb in a comforting caress. "I don't know what it's like to be fat. But it's not fair to frame your struggles as if no one else can comprehend them. To deliberately shut me out solely because I have a few strands of DNA that put my face together like this."

He circled an index finger over his cheekbones, and the darkness underneath the motion, in his expression, startled her.

"I'm not trying to shut you out." Was she?

The alternative meant she'd have to let him glimpse her innermost secrets, her deepest fears. It would mean trusting him with far more than her body. It would mean trusting him with her soul.

But hadn't she already done that when she invited him into her bed?

"You may not be consciously trying to. But you

are," he said mildly. "And not only that, you're making an assumption about me based on my appearance. Like I can't possibly know what it feels like to have disappointments or pain because of the way I look."

Speechless, she stared into his snapping, smoky eyes. She'd hurt him with her thoughtless comments.

She *had* made assumptions and drawn her fat-girl self around her like a familiar, impenetrable blanket.

Dax had called it during their discussion on the park bench. She ran screaming in the other direction before a man could get close enough to hurt her.

Had she already screwed this up—whatever *this* was—before it started?

"I'm sorry," she said sincerely and squeezed his hand. He squeezed back and her heart lightened a little. "I'm sensitive about food and about being fat. It's an ugly part of me. I'm not used to sharing it with anyone."

"There's nothing ugly about you," he shot right back. "Why in the world would you think a few pounds makes you ugly?"

She debated. It was so much easier to make a

joke. But she'd been patiently explaining the components of happily ever after to Dax for weeks, which had everything to do with honesty, vulnerability and trust. Was she really going to balk when it was her turn to lay it all out?

"You've seen my mother. You've been in that world. Surely the pursuit of thinness is not so mysterious an ideal."

He shrugged. "But you're not a model. Neither are you your mother. So your weight is not a requirement for your job."

Easy for him to say. It was different for boys no matter what they looked like.

"It's not that simple. I grew up surrounded by swans and constantly aware I wasn't one of them. In case I didn't feel bad enough about being overweight, my mother made sure I didn't forget it for a moment."

"She's the one who made you self-conscious about being fat?" Dax scowled. "That's horrible."

His unconditional support squeezed her heart sweetly. "It turned out okay. I buried myself in algorithms and computer code instead of hanging out in the spotlight, which was, and still is, cruel. I built a business born out of the desire to shut myself away from all the negativity. Only EA International could have gotten me in front of those cameras where we met. Even now, I give deserving women makeovers because I know how it feels to be in the middle of all those swans, with no one on your side."

"I'm glad you found the fortitude to venture onto my set." Dax smiled. "And I like that you made something positive out of a bad experience."

"There's more." And it was the really important part. "That's why my profile questions dig into the heart of who you are. So my clients can find someone to love them for what's underneath, not what they look like."

Which was not-so-coincidentally what she wanted too—someone to love her forever, no matter what. She'd never had that before.

The smile slipped from his face and he gazed at her solemnly. "I get that."

Of course he did. She'd made sweeping generalizations about him because of his appearance and she'd bet it wasn't the first time someone had done that. Not only did he understand the point about loving someone's insides; of all the people she'd shared her philosophy with, he had the singular distinction of being the only one who'd seen the pain that had created it.

And she was terrified of what he'd do with all this insight.

Eleven

Dax took Elise to eat at the top of Reunion Tower, a place she'd never been despite having lived in Dallas for years. They dined while overlooking the downtown area as the room revolved 360 degrees inside the ball. It should have been a wildly romantic evening.

It *was*. But Elise couldn't quite relax.

When they returned to her house from dinner, Dax took her keys and opened the front door for her, then swept her up in his arms to carry her over the threshold. Solid and strong, he maneuvered through the door frame without hesitation, and it was undeniably sexy.

"What's this all about?" she asked as soon as she unstuck her tongue from the roof of her mouth.

"I seem to have a lot of trouble getting past your front door. This way, I'm guaranteed entrance." He grinned at her cockeyed stare. "Plus, I've got a very special treat planned and thought I'd start it off with a bang."

"Really?" Her curiosity was piqued as her tension lessened. "What is it?"

He let her slide to the ground braced against his gorgeous body and took her hand. "Follow me, Ms. Arundel, and see for yourself."

That made her grin, dispelling more of her strange mood. She trailed him upstairs and the second she entered the bedroom, he whirled her into a mind-numbing kiss.

Her brain emptied as his lips devoured her and heat tunneled into every last crevice of her body. *Oh, yes.*

Bright, white-hot desire flared in a sunburst at her core, soaking her in need and flooding her with Dax, and she couldn't catch her breath. She wanted him to love her exactly as he had last night, perfectly, completely.

Slowly, he backed her to the bed and when she would have stumbled, he tightened his arms. Then he sat her down and drew off her boots, one zipper at a time, and kissed her uncovered calves, all the way to her heels.

She watched him through heavy eyelids, a little unable to process the sight of such a beautiful man at her feet, all his attention on her. He glanced up, his gaze full of dark, sinful promise, and she shuddered as he centered himself between her legs.

With deft, strong fingers, he gathered the hem of her dress and slowly worked it up over her thighs, caressing her bare skin as he went, following the fabric with his mouth and tongue.

A moan rose in her throat and she strangled on it as he licked at her nub through her damp panties.

"I want to see you, Elise," he murmured and slipped off her dress with skill. Quick-like-fox, he had her bra and panties in the same pile as her dress.

As he raked her with a smoldering, hungry once-over, she fought the urge to crawl under the covers.

"You are so beautiful," he croaked, as though he might be coming down with something. Or she'd affected him enough to clog his throat.

Wasn't that amazing? *She* affected *him.*

He stared down at her as he lowered himself to

the bed next to her, still fully clothed. "I want to make you feel beautiful."

"You do," she said automatically. Well, actually, he made her feel good. Beautiful was a little more difficult to come by.

His brows arched. "Maybe. But I can do better. Much better. So tonight is about that."

He reached under a pillow and withdrew a bag of Ghirardelli chocolate chips. She'd recognize the bag a mile away. Her mouth started watering. And then her brain caught up. "Why is that instrument of torture in my bed?"

Dax grinned and winked. "You told me you liked chocolate. *Voilà*. We'll get to the shoes another time."

The wall her insides had thrown up crumbled and everything went liquid. "You were paying attention to what I said?"

"Of course." He scowled in confusion. "Why would I have asked if I didn't want to know the answer?"

Heat flamed through her cheeks and she shut her eyes. "I thought you were being polite."

Laughing, he kissed both of her shut eyelids in succession until she opened them. "One thing I am not is polite. But I am interested in giving you an amazing experience. Starting now."

With a wicked smile, he laid her back and tore open the bag, spilling chocolate chips all over her bare stomach.

The chips rolled everywhere, and she jackknifed automatically to catch them, but he stopped her with a gentle hand to her shoulder. Then he grasped a piece of chocolate between his fingertips and traced it between her breasts, up her throat and to her lips, teasing her with it.

The rich, sweet smell of chocolate drugged her senses. She wanted to eat that bite of heaven in the worst way. But she couldn't. A moment on the lips…and it went straight to her hips. She didn't keep chocolate in the house for a reason.

"Open," he instructed. "None of these calories count because honey, I promise you're about to burn them all."

The temptation was humongous. She wrestled with it. And lost.

How could she do anything else but eat it? Chocolate burst on her tongue and a moment later, his tongue twined with hers, tasting the chocolate along with her in a delicious kiss.

The twin sensations of Dax and chocolate nearly

pushed her over the edge. She moaned in appreciation. Desire. Surrender.

Trailing chocolate kisses back down her throat, he paused to line up several chips around her nipple and proceeded to lick each one, smearing more chocolate on her breasts than he got in his mouth. He proceeded to suck off the sweetness, sending her into a taut spiral of need that could only be salved one way.

As if he'd read her mind again, he lowered himself between her thighs, opened them and kissed each one. Muscles tight with anticipation, she choked on a breath, waiting for the sweet fire of his intimate kiss.

He didn't disappoint her. She felt a chip graze her nub and then Dax's tongue followed it, and her eyelids slammed closed as her senses pulsed with pleasure.

"You taste delicious," he rasped and stuck another chip under his tongue, laving so hard, she came instantly in a starburst of sparkles that bowed her back and ripped a cry from her throat.

Immediately, he rose up and treated her to a chocolate, musky kiss, twining all the flavors together into an overwhelming, sensual bouquet.

"See how delicious you taste?" he murmured and

cupped her with his hand, sliding fingers through her folds and into her damp center, yanking yet another climax from deep inside.

Still in the throes of a chocolate orgasm, she couldn't sort one sensation from the other and didn't want to. Finally the ripples faded, leaving her gasping and nearly blind as dots crowded her vision.

"Delicious," he repeated. "Beautiful."

Then he put the icing on it.

"By the way," he said casually. "In case it wasn't crystal clear, this was me showing you how gorgeous you are. Remember this every time you put chocolate in your mouth, which better be a lot. Because I don't want you to ever, ever forget that you're beautiful or that the sight of you eating chocolate is so hot, I'm about to lose it."

She blinked and focused on his wolfish smile. He'd been trying to psychoanalyze her with this little stunt?

So now every time she thought about chocolate, she'd make all kinds of associations that it should never have, like unbelievable pleasure, a gorgeous man's mouth tasting of sin and sugar, and the pièce de résistance, that watching her eat chocolate turned him on.

It was...brilliant. The benefits of sleeping with a man who understood both psychology and a woman's body couldn't be overstated.

And she wasn't simply falling for him; it was more like being dropped off a cliff, straight into a mess of emotion she had no idea how to handle.

She would have thought herself capable of understanding love, if indeed that's what was going on. Certainly she would have said she could recognize it. And it did not resemble this crazy, upside-down thing inside that was half thrilling, half terrifying and 100 percent Dax.

What if this *wasn't* love but an orgasm-induced hallucination? Worse, what if she went with it, straight into a broken heart? Her fat-girl blanket usually kept that from happening, but she'd lost it.

Or rather, Dax had stolen it from her with chocolate.

And he'd completely piqued her curiosity as to what he planned to do with shoes.

Dax picked up Elise and took her to the bathroom, where he filled the tub and spent a long time washing the chocolate from her body. He wanted to sink into the steaming water and sink into Elise, but he was too busy breathing her in to stop.

She smelled like chocolate and well-loved woman and home, all rolled into one bundle he could not get enough of. He'd only meant to worship her gorgeous body and enable her to eat something she liked at the same time. He had *not* intended to forever alter his perception of chocolate, but he'd never taste it again without getting a hard-on.

Which wasn't necessarily a bad thing.

Finally he couldn't stand being separated from her any longer and stripped to slide into the tub. She watched him unashamedly, ravenous gaze flickering to his rigid erection as he bared it. Last night she'd had a hard time with that, as if nakedness were shocking.

Not so tonight. But he didn't dare say he was proud of her lest he frighten her back into that shell. Besides, the heat in her eyes sent such a shaft of desire spiking through him, he couldn't do anything other than slide into the tub, gather her against his chest and dive in.

He kissed her, openmouthed, sloppy and so very raw. She melted into him, fitting her lithe body into his. Water sloshed out of the tub, which she didn't notice and he didn't point out.

He needed her. Now.

After an eternity of fumbling due to wet fingers and wet body parts and far too much "help" from Elise that nearly set off what would be a nuclear explosion of a release, Dax got the condom in place.

He never had this much trouble. But his fingers were still shaking as he slid into her with a groan and then he simply clung, hands gripping Elise's shoulders. Flinging his head back, he let the sensations bleed through him and only some of them were physical.

That profound sense of what he could only label as *happiness* saturated the experience, lighting him up inside. It felt as if it would burst from his skin and pour out in a river. He savored the harmony, the rightness of it.

Elise, clearly impatient with all the savoring, planted her knees on either side of him and took over the rhythm, and he let her because it was amazing. The faster she moved, the higher he soared, and a growl ripped from his mouth unrestrained as she pushed him to the edge.

Nearly incoherent and almost numb with the effort to hold back, he fingered her in an intimate caress, silently begging her to let go. Instantly, she tightened around him in an answering pulse that triggered his release, and he came in a fountain of blessed relief.

She slumped on his chest, cheek to his skin, and he shut his eyes, reveling in the boneless bliss that he'd only ever experienced at the hands of Elise.

Being with her evoked so many things he had no way to describe, things he hoped never went away. But since he didn't know how it had happened in the first place, what guarantee did he have he wouldn't wake up tomorrow and find himself back in the real world where Elise wasn't "the one"?

Because here in this alternate reality he'd somehow fallen into, it felt an awful lot as though she was a…soul mate.

Against all odds, he wanted to believe the concept existed, that it might be possible for him. For them.

After they dried off and got comfortably snugged together in bed he murmured, "Elise, you have to promise me something."

"Anything. After the chocolate, you name it." She sighed, her breath teasing the hair on his torso.

"Don't stop. Keep doing whatever you're doing and don't stop. Even if I tell you to."

She stirred and raised her head to peer at him in the darkened room, lit only by the moonlight pouring in through the opened blinds. "Why would you tell me to?"

"Because..."

I'm broken.

That's why he'd never found a woman worth promising forever to. Why Elise's matchmaking efforts had failed, despite participating in her profile sessions to the best of his ability. Not because there was something wrong with the women he'd dated, or even Candy, but because something was wrong with him. How could he explain that he pushed women away on purpose, before things got complicated?

But then, he didn't have to explain. Elise knew that already. She had spelled it out in painful detail on the park bench. If he was being honest, that had been the tipping point, the moment he knew she'd snared an unrecoverable piece of him he'd never meant to give up.

He tried again. "Because I'm..."

Falling for you.

His eyelids slammed shut in frustration and fear and God knew what else. What was wrong with him that he couldn't voice a simple sentence to tell this amazing woman how she made him feel? Or at least confess that she made him want to be better than he'd ever dreamed possible?

He wanted to be the man she deserved. For the first time in his life, he didn't want to push her away.

But he knew he was going to anyway.

He couldn't say all those things because Elise wasn't *his* soul mate. She was someone else's and he was in the way. For her sake, he would have to end things eventually.

That realization nearly split him in two. Appropriate to be as broken on the outside as he was on the inside.

"Hey." Her soft hand cupped his jaw and her thumb rested near his eyes, brushing the lashes until he opened them. "What's going on? You're never at a loss for words."

He laughed in spite of himself. She'd been tying him up in knots from day one. Why should this be any different?

"Yeah, this is all kinds of abnormal."

"Start with that. What's abnormal, being in bed together?" She cocked her head and smoothed the sheets over them. "Are you about to tell me your reputation with women is vastly inflated? Because

I won't believe you. The things you do to me can only be the result of years of careful study."

"I've had a lot of sex, Elise. Make no mistake," he said without apology. "But it wasn't anything like this. What's different is you. I can't explain it. It feels…bigger. Stronger. I don't know what to do with it."

She stared at him, wide-eyed. "Really? It's not like this with other women?"

"Not even close. I didn't know it *could* be different."

If he had, he would have hunted down Elise Arundel about a decade ago. Maybe if he had, before he'd become so irrevocably damaged, things might have worked out between them.

He could have actually *been* the man she needed instead of merely wanting to be.

Wanting wasn't good enough. She deserved someone unbroken and he needed to give her space to find that guy.

But it didn't have to be now. He could wait a few days, or maybe longer.

"But I'm just me." Bewilderment crept over her face. "I'm not doing anything special."

"You don't have to do anything special. It just is. You don't feel it, too?"

Slowly, she nodded and a sense of relief burst through his gut. Relief that this wasn't all one-sided. Guilt because it might already be too late to get out without hurting her.

"I feel it. It scares me and I don't know why." She gripped his hand. "It's not supposed to be like this, all mixed up, and like I can't breathe if you're gone. Like I can't breathe when you're here."

Exactly. That's how he'd felt all week as he'd talked to the couples Elise had matched and then drove around aimlessly, out of sorts, with no clue how to absolve the riot of stuff seething under his skin. Elise was his affliction. And his deliverance.

Maybe she was the answer, the only woman in existence who could fix him. If he wasn't broken anymore, maybe he could find a way to be with Elise forever. Maybe he *could* have her, without pushing her away. But only if he could finally let her behind his curtain.

"I have to tell you something," he said before he lost his nerve. "Your mother made you feel bad about your weight. Well, I understand how mothers can shape your entire outlook on life. Because mine left. When I was seven."

Tears pricked at his eyelids. He'd never spoken

of his mother's abandonment and somehow, saying it aloud made it An Issue.

"Oh, honey, I'm so sorry." Elise pressed her lips to his temple and just held him without another word. The odd, bright happiness she evoked filled him.

"It's stupid to still let it affect me. I know that," he muttered and let his muscles relax. He wouldn't flee into the night and not talk about this.

Elise, of all people, understood the twisted, sometimes warped pathways of his mind, often when he didn't get it himself. He could trust her.

"Dax." She gave him time to collect himself and that small act meant a lot to him. "If you don't want to let it affect you, then stop."

"Oh, sure. I'll wave my magic wand and everything will be fine. Better yet, why don't you wave yours?" he said magnanimously. She didn't laugh.

Instead, she leaned forward and pierced him with a somber gaze. "That's exactly what I've been trying to do. By matching you with your soul mate, so you could be happy with someone. I want that for you."

"What if I said I want that too?"

Twelve

She froze, confusion flitting through her expression. "You do?"

"Yeah. Maybe."

She blinked and swallowed several times in a row before speaking. "You mean commitment, emotions, forever?"

Hope shone in her eyes.

For a brief moment, he felt an answering tug of hope in his heart. Forever sounded amazing.

And then reality took over and squelched everything good inside. These feelings would change—or fade—and he'd prove he was just like his mother by walking out the door.

He was wrong for Elise. She had all these visions

of true love he could never measure up to. Being with her made him want things he couldn't have, and it wasn't her job to fix him.

That was the final nail. Just because he wanted to be unbroken didn't make it so. Why hadn't he kept his mouth shut and his curtain closed? He couldn't continue this charade, as though there was a future for them.

For once, he'd thought about trying. That's why he'd shared the truth with her. That's why he'd gotten out of the car.

He shouldn't have. And he had a hundred reasons why he should walk out right now before it was too late. He wasn't cut out for this, for relationships. He had to get out now, before he hurt her even more later.

Ruthlessly, he shut off everything inside, especially the part that had started to believe.

"Why do you sound so stunned?" he said instead of answering her question as he scrambled for a way to let her down easy. "This is your area of expertise. Didn't you set out to change my mind about love?"

"I'm not that good," she blurted out and bit her lip.

"Of course you are. The couples you matched

think you're every bit the magical fairy godmother you claimed. Take credit where credit is due."

A grin spilled onto her face. "Does that mean I won the wager?"

His chest had the weight of a skyscraper on it and all Elise could think about was the wager? "The wager is over."

"Sorry." Her confusion wrapped around him, increasing the tension unbearably. "What about marriage? Are you on board with that, too?"

The longer he dragged this out, the more hope she'd gather. Heart bleeding, he shrugged and looked away. "Maybe someday. With the right woman."

"Wait a minute." Unease flitting over her face, she sat up, clutching the covers to her bare breasts. "I thought you were talking about having a rela-tionship with *me*."

Carefully, he composed his expression as if this was no more than a negotiation gone wrong and both parties just needed to walk away amicably.

It nearly killed him.

"Come on, Elise. You and I both know we won't work. I got out of the car because I knew I was missing something and I needed you to tell me what. So thanks. I'm good."

She wasn't buying it. Elise was far too sharp to be put off by half truths. That's why it never paid to let anyone behind the curtain.

"Dax, we have something good. Don't you want to see if we work before giving up?"

Her warm hand on his arm shouldn't have felt so right, as though his skin had been crafted specifically for her touch.

"It doesn't matter what I want. I can't make long-term promises. To anyone," he stressed. "I'm all about keeping my word because my mother didn't. I can't stand the thought of caring about someone and then figuring out I don't have what it takes to stick around."

Nothing like the whole truth to make the point. She needed to understand that this was for her own good, so she could move on and find her Mr. Forever, and he could go back to his empty loft.

"But you can make promises to me because I'm your soul mate."

The soft whisper penetrated his misery. "What did you say?"

"*I'm* your soul mate. Your perfect woman. The computer matched us."

Something dark whirled through his chest,

squeezing it even tighter, pushing air from his lungs. "That's not true. It matched me with Candy."

She shook her head. "My name came up first. But I thought I'd made a mistake due to the unorthodox profile sessions. So I messed around with the responses until Candy's name came up instead."

Blood rushed to his head and the back of his neck heated. "You did *what?*"

"It was the ethical thing to do. I thought I'd compromised the results because of how I felt about you."

Ethical. He'd been told Candy was his soul mate and therefore he'd believed Elise was meant for someone else. But it had never felt right, never fit... because he'd thought *he* was the problem.

Instead, it was all a lie.

Letting him think he couldn't do happily ever after, letting him think he was broken—that was her definition of *ethical?*

"Let me get this straight." He pinched the bridge of his nose and reeled his temper back. "You had such deep feelings for me it compelled you to match me with someone who isn't my soul mate?"

"I hoped you'd hit it off. Because I do want you to be happy. Candy just wasn't right for you."

"And who is, you?"

The question was delivered so scathingly, she flinched and didn't respond. Fortunately. His mood had degenerated to the point where he was genuinely afraid of what he might say.

He rolled from the bed and scouted around until he found his pants, and then jerked them on, but stood staring at the wall, fists clenched until he thought he could speak rationally.

"Why tell me now? Why didn't you tell me from the beginning?"

The wager. She'd been trying to win and altered the results in order to do so. It was the only explanation. That's why she'd asked if she'd won earlier. Rage boiled up again, clouding his vision.

"It wasn't a secret," she said defensively. "I thought you'd laugh and make some smarmy joke about how I couldn't possibly resist you. Plus, I wanted you to have a shot at finding your real soul mate."

"Who isn't you."

She couldn't be. His real soul mate wouldn't have let him believe all this time that he was the problem. That he was the broken one and that's why Elise's algorithm couldn't find his perfect match.

He'd trusted her. In vain, apparently.

If she'd just told him the truth, everything might

be different. But she'd stolen that chance and thoroughly destroyed his fledgling belief in the possibility of happily ever after.

"I am," she corrected softly. "My match process just realized it before I did."

"Pardon me for questioning the results when it seems your process is a little, shall we say, subjective. In fact, I'd say this whole wager was slanted from the beginning. So save the sales pitch, babe."

Oh, he'd been so blind. From the very first moment, all she'd cared about was proving to everyone that she could change his mind about relationships. She didn't want true love, or at least not with him. It had all been an act to gain the upper hand. If Dax had one talent, it was recognizing a good show when he saw one.

"Slanted? What are you talking about?"

"Admit it. This was all an attempt to bring me to my knees, wasn't it? You planned for it to happen this way." He shook his head and laughed contemptuously. "You're far, far better at this than I ever dreamed. To think I almost fell for it."

She'd dug into his psyche with no other intent than to uncover his deepest longings and use them against him. It was unforgivable.

The only bright spot in this nightmare was that

he no longer had to worry about how to push her away or whether he'd eventually walk out the door. She'd destroyed their relationship all on her own.

Thankfully, he'd found out the truth before it was too late.

His mistake had been starting to trust her, even a little.

"Fell for what? Dax, you're not making any sense."

Pulse hammering, Elise sorted through the conversation to figure out where this had gotten so mixed up. What had she missed? Up until now, she'd always been able to sort his fact from fiction, especially when he tried to throw up smoke screens, but that ability had disappeared long about midnight yesterday.

She was losing him, losing all the ground she'd gained—or imagined she'd gained. Clearly, he'd done some kind of about-face but apparently not in her direction. That couldn't be right. She couldn't be this close to getting a man like Dax for her own and not figure out how to get her happily ever after.

He shook his head and laughed again without any humor. "All this time I thought *you* were looking for a relationship and I *wasn't*. You sat right there on that park bench and told me exactly what you wanted. I ignored it." He crossed the room and poked a rigid finger in her face. "'I want to beat you at your own game,' you said. And you know what, you almost did."

She flinched automatically. Oh, God. She had said that. But the way he'd twisted it around…unbelievable. As if she'd cold-bloodedly planned this to hurt him, playing dirty, fast and loose.

"Listen, this wasn't the game I was trying to win."

Except she'd been pretty focused on winning. From the beginning. Maybe she'd been more compromised than she'd assumed. She'd developed feelings for him without really understanding how to love him.

Maybe she didn't really understand male/female dynamics unless they were other people's.

"What game *were* you trying to win, then? Why is this a game at all?" A dangerous glint in his eye warned her to let him finish before she leaped on the defensive again. "Tread carefully, Elise. You clearly have no idea what you're playing around with here."

"This isn't a game," she cried. "When my name came up as your match, I wanted it to be true. I wanted you for myself and I thought those feelings compromised my integrity."

"You're lying." The harsh lines of his face convicted her further. "If that was true, you wouldn't have played so hard to get."

She couldn't fault his logic. Except he was drawing the wrong conclusion. "The truth is I didn't believe I was enough to change your mind about happily ever after."

"Enough?" he spat. "Enough what?"

"Pretty enough, good enough, thin enough. Take your pick," she whispered.

He laughed again and the sound skated down her spine. "I get it now. You said you don't trust easily, but in reality, you don't trust at all. You didn't ever intend to give me a real chance, did you? That's the game you wanted to beat me at. Get me to confess my feelings and then take my legs out from under me. Good job."

"I *did* want to give you a chance. You said we wouldn't work."

He threw his hands up. "This is why I don't do relationships. This conversation is like a vicious circle. With teeth."

She cursed as she realized her mistake. Misdirection was his forte and he was such a master, she'd almost missed it. He *had* developed feelings for her and they scared him. That's what all this was. Smoke and mirrors to deflect from what was going on back stage.

This was the part where she needed to tread carefully.

"Last night," she whispered. "Before you kissed me. You said you meant it. What did you mean?"

The raw vulnerability in his expression took her breath. And when her lungs finally filled, they ached with the effort.

"I meant I was falling in love with you." His expression darkened as her heart tripped dangerously. "I—forget it. It's too late to have that conversation now."

Dax was falling in love with her? The revelation pinged through her mind, through her heart—painfully—because he'd finally laid it all out there while also telling her to forget it. As if she could.

She'd done it. She'd reversed his stance on love and happily ever after. Shannon Elise Arundel *was* that good. Her match program was foolproof. The algorithm had matched them because she had a unique ability to understand him, to see the real him, just as he did her.

Why hadn't she realized it sooner?

"It's not too late." She crawled to her knees, begging him without words for something she had no idea how to express. "Let's figure this out."

"I don't want to figure it out!" He huffed out a frustrated breath. "Elise, I thought I was *broken*. That the reason you couldn't find my soul mate was because there was something wrong with me. I felt guilty for wanting you when your soul mate was supposed to be someone else, someone better. Instead, you were lying all along. You never trusted me."

In one shot, he'd blown all the smoke away and told her the absolute unvarnished truth. While she'd been pushing him away, he'd filed the rejection under *it's not her, it's me.*

Speechless, she stared at the pain-carved lines in his beautiful face. "I didn't know that's how you'd take it when I told you I was your match. There's nothing wrong with you. This is all about me and my issues."

"I get that you have a problem believing I think you're beautiful." He snorted. "You want to find true love but you won't let anyone in long enough to trust that they love you. That's why you've never had a connection with anyone."

"I've been holding out for someone to love me. The real me, underneath."

I've been holding out for you.

He swept her with an angry look. "Yet you're completely hung up on whether you're beautiful enough. If someone loves you solely for what you look like, that's not true love. Neither is it love to refuse to trust. You have a lot of nerve preaching to me about something you know nothing about."

"You're right." Head bowed, she admitted the absolute, unvarnished truth in kind. "I didn't fully trust you. I don't know how."

"I bought into what you were selling." His bleak voice scored her heart. "Hook, line and sinker. I wanted something more than sex. Understanding. Support. A connection."

Everything she'd hoped for. For both of them. But somehow she'd messed up. "I want those things, too."

A tear tracked down her cheek and he watched it. As it fell to the bed, he shook his head. "You're not capable of giving me those things. This is over, if it ever started in the first place. I can't do this."

Then he stormed from the room, snagging his bag on the way out. She let him go, too numb to figure out how to fix it. Some relationship expert she was.

Dax's ex-girlfriends had been wrong. He wasn't cold and heartless and he hadn't screwed Elise over. She'd done it to him, smashing his fragile feelings into unrecoverable pieces because at the end of the day, she hadn't trusted Dax enough to believe he could really love her. She hadn't trusted herself enough to tell him they'd been matched. And now it was too late to do it all over.

Happily ever after might very well be a myth after all. And if that was true, where did that leave her and Dax? Or her company?

The sound of the front door slamming reverberated in her frozen heart.

Dax nearly took out a row of mailboxes in his haste to speed away from the mistake in his rearview mirror. Astounding how he'd assumed he was the broken one in their relationship. Only to discover she was far more broken.

While he'd naively been trying to get out without hurting her, she'd actually been one step ahead of him the entire time, determined to break him. And she'd done a hell of a job. She'd matched him with the perfect woman all right—the only one capable of getting under his skin and destroying everything in her path.

It was late, but Wakefield Media did not sleep. He drove to the office, determined not to think. Or to feel. He closed it all off through sheer will until the only thing left was a strange hardness in his chest that made it impossible to catch a deep breath.

Shutting himself off behind his desk, Dax dove into the business he loved, the only thing he could really depend on. This company he'd built from the ground up was his happily ever after, the only one available to him. If he put his head down, maybe he'd come out the other side with some semblance of normality. Dawn came and went but the hardness in his chest didn't fade.

At noon, he'd had no human contact other than a brief nod to Patricia as she dropped off a cup of coffee several hours ago. Fatigue dragged at him. Well, that and a heavy heart.

His phone beeped and he checked it automatically. Elise. He deleted the text message without reading it, just as he'd done with the other three. There was nothing she could say that he wanted to hear.

Morosely, he swiveled his chair to stare out over

the Dallas skyline and almost involuntarily, his eye was drawn to the building directly across from him, where Reynolds Capital Management used to reside. Dax had heard that Leo left the venture capital game and had gone into business with Tommy Garrett, a whiz kid inventor.

It was crazy and so unlike Leo. They'd been friends for a long time—until Daniella had come along and upset the status quo.

Bad, bad subject. The hardness in his chest started to hurt and the urge to punch something grew until he couldn't physically sit at his desk any longer.

He sent Patricia an instant message asking for the address of Garrett-Reynolds Engineering and the second he got it, he strode to his car. It was time to have it out with Leo once and for all.

Except Leo wasn't at the office. Dax eyed Tommy Garrett, whom he'd met at a party an eon ago. The kid still looked as though he belonged on a surfboard instead of in a boardroom.

"Sorry, dude," Tommy said and stuck a Doritos chip in his mouth. "Leo's still on vacation. But I'm pretty sure he's at home now if you want to catch him there."

"Thanks." Dax went back to his car, still shaking his head. Leo—at home in the middle of the day on a Monday. His affliction with Daniella was even worse than Dax had imagined.

By the time he hit Leo's driveway, Dax was good and worked up. This time, he didn't hesitate, but drove right up to the gate and rolled down his window so the security system could grant him entrance.

Leo was waiting for him on the front steps as Dax swung out of the Audi. Of course the state-of-the-art security system had alerted the Reynoldses that they had a visitor, and clearly Leo was as primed for a throw down as Dax was. Dax meant to give it to him.

"Dax." Leo smiled warmly, looking well-rested, tan and not wearing a suit. "It's good to see you. I'm glad you came by."

Dax did a double take.

Who was this guy? Because he didn't resemble the Leo Dax knew.

"Hi," Dax muttered, and tried to orient. Leo wasn't supposed to be happy. And he wasn't supposed to be nice. They weren't friends anymore.

"Please, come in." Leo jerked his head behind him toward the house. "Dannie's pouring us some iced tea."

"This isn't a social call," he fairly snarled and then heard himself. Where were his manners?

Leo didn't flinch. "I didn't assume that it was. But this is my home, and my wife wanted to serve you a drink. It's what civilized people do when someone comes by without an invitation."

My wife. The dividing line couldn't have been clearer. But then, Leo had drawn that line back in his office when he'd told Dax in no uncertain terms that Daniella was more important to him than anything, including money, the deal between Leo and Dax, and even their friendship.

All at once, Dax wanted to know why.

"I'm sorry," Dax said sincerely. "Tea is great. Thanks."

He followed Leo into a dappled sunroom with a view of the windswept back acreage of the property. The branches were bare of leaves this late into the season, save a few evergreens dotting the landscape.

Daniella bustled in with a tray, smiled at Dax and set a glass full of amber liquid in front of each man. "Nice to see you, Dax. Enjoy. I'll make myself scarce."

Gracious as always. Even to a man who made no secret of his intense dislike and mistrust of her.

Dax watched her drop a kiss on Leo's head. He snagged her hand to keep her in place, then returned the kiss on her lips, exchanging a private smile that seemed like a language all its own. They were so obviously in love, it poleaxed Dax right in the heart.

Because he didn't have that. Nor did he hold any hope of having it.

Against everything he'd ever believed about himself, the world and how he fit into it, he wanted what Leo and Daniella had.

The floodgates had been opened and then shut so swiftly, he'd barely had time to acclimate, to figure out what he was going to do with all the emotions he'd never felt before. Then *bam!* Betrayal at its finest. The two people he'd let himself care about had *both* betrayed him. And one of them would answer for it right now.

After Daniella disappeared, Dax faced Leo squarely. "I suppose you're wondering why I'm here."

"Not really." Leo grinned at Dax's raised eyebrows. "Dannie and Elise are very good friends. I'm guessing you didn't know that."

Elise. Her name pierced that hard place in his chest and nearly finished what the lovey-dovey scene between Leo and Daniella had started. Death by emotion. It seemed fitting somehow.

And no, he hadn't realized Daniella and Elise were friends. Daniella had probably been treated to an earful already this morning. "And your wife tells you everything, right?"

"Yep."

Dax sank down in the wicker chair, but it didn't swallow him as he would have preferred. If he'd known his spectacular flameout at the hands of Elise had been trotted out for everyone's amusement, he might have gone someplace else, like Timbuktu.

"Last night was really messed up," Dax allowed without really meaning to. It just came out.

"I sympathize." Leo cleared his throat. "Which is more than you did for me when I was going through something similar, I might add."

That hurt. "Is this what you were going through? Because I don't see how that's possible."

Leo and Daniella had an effortless relationship, as if they'd been born for each other and never questioned whether they trusted the other.

"No, it's not the same because we're different people in love with very different women."

"I'm not in love with Elise," Dax broke in.

He might have been entertaining the notion, but she'd killed it. Somehow it was worse to finally embrace the idea that love wasn't just a fairy tale only to have your heart smashed.

Leo just looked at him and smirked. "And that's your problem right there. Denial. That, plus an inability to give someone a chance."

"That's not true," he burst out. "She's the one who didn't give me a chance. She lied to me. I can't trust anyone."

And that was the really painful part. There wasn't one single person in existence he could fully trust. If it could have been anyone, he'd have put his money on Elise, the one person who understood the man behind the curtain. He *had* put his money on Elise—five hundred thousand dollars—and she'd never lost sight of the prize. He should take a lesson.

"I can give you relationship advice all day long if that's what you're after. But you didn't really come here to find out that you guard yourself by pushing people away? You already know that."

Yeah, he did. He ended relationships before he got invested. He left women before they could hurt him. No mystery there. The question was why he'd let his guard down with Elise in the first place.

Dax sipped his tea and decided to go for broke with Leo. "I came to find out why Daniella was such a big deal. I know you married her. But why her? What was special about her?"

Leo's face lit up. "I love her. That alone makes her special. But I love her because she makes me whole. She allows me to be me. She *enables* me to be me. And I wake up every day wanting to do the same for her. That's why Elise matched us. Because we're soul mates."

Dax nearly snorted but caught himself. The evidence stood for itself and there was no need to act cynical about it any longer. No one in this room was confused about whether he believed in it. But believing in soul mates and allowing a woman who professed to be yours to take a fillet knife to your heart were two different things.

"And that was worth ending a friendship over?" Dax asked.

Stupid question. Clearly Leo thought so and at that particular moment, Dax almost didn't blame him. Look what Leo had gotten in return.

"Dax." Leo sat forward in his chair. "I didn't end our friendship. You did. You weren't being a friend when you said disparaging things about my wife. You weren't being a friend when you demanded

I choose you over her. I was messed up, wondering how I could love my wife and still maintain the workaholic life I thought I wanted. I needed a friend. Where were you?"

There was no censure in Leo's tone. But there should have been. Hearing it spelled out like that sheared a new layer of skin off Dax's already-raw wounds. He'd been a crappy friend yet Leo had welcomed Dax into his home without question.

"I was wallowing in my own selfishness," Dax muttered. "I was a jerk. I'm sorry."

"It's okay. It was okay as soon as you rolled up the driveway. I've been waiting for you to come by." Leo held out his hand for Dax to shake, which he did without hesitation.

The hardness in his chest lifted a bit. "Thanks for not barring the gate."

"No problem. I had a feeling you'd need a friend after what happened with Elise. It sounded rough. I'd like to hear about it from you, though."

Dax watched a bird hop from branch to bare branch outside the sunroom's glass walls. "Her computer program matched us. But she wasn't interested in me or finding the love of her life. Or professional ethics. Just winning."

"I watched the interview," Leo said quietly. "You

were ruthless. Can you blame her for bringing her A game?"

The interview. It felt like a lifetime ago, back when he'd been smugly certain he couldn't lose the bet because love didn't exist. He almost preferred it when he'd still believed that.

"She screwed me over. I can't forget that."

"You reap what you sow. You started out going head-to-head and that's where you ended up. Change it if that's not what you want."

Leo sipped his tea as Dax shifted uncomfortably. "You say that like I had some fault in this, too."

"Don't you?" Leo tilted his head in way that told Dax the question was rhetorical. "I went into my marriage with Dannie assuming I wanted a wife who took care of my house and left me alone. And that's what I got until I realized it wasn't what I really wanted. Fortunately, she was waiting for me to wake up and see what I had. You didn't give Elise that chance. You ended it."

Of course he'd ended it. "I don't make promises I can't keep."

It was an automatic response, one he'd always said was the reason he didn't do relationships. But that wasn't why he'd walked out on Elise.

The problem was greater than the fear of learning he was like his mother, faithless and unable to make promises to one person forever.

He also feared being like his father—pathetic. Mooning over a woman who didn't actually care about him, waiting in vain for her to come back.

Elise hadn't told him the truth and he could never trust her to stay. And if he let himself love her, and she didn't stay, he'd be doomed to a lifetime of pain and an eternity of solitude because he'd never get over losing his soul mate.

Thirteen

When the doorbell rang, Elise's pulse sprang into double time as she flew to answer it.

Dax.

He'd come to apologize, talk, yell at her. She didn't care. Anything was fine as long as he was here. Hungry to see him again after three miserable days, she swung open the door.

Her heart plummeted.

It was Dannie, dressed to the nines in a gorgeous winter-white cashmere coat, matching skirt and heels. Next to her stood Juliet, the new princess of Delamer, wearing a T-shirt and jeans, of course.

"What are you doing here?" Elise glowered at Juliet. "You're supposed to be on your honeymoon."

The princess shrugged delicately and waved a hand full of bitten-off nails. "It was a working honeymoon and you need me more than His Royal Highness. I left my husband in New York with a host of boring European diplomats. I miss him already, but I owe you more than I can ever repay for giving me back the love of my life."

"I need you?" Elise glanced at Dannie. "You called Juliet and told her I needed her?"

"Yes, yes I did." Dannie bustled Juliet into the house, followed her and shut the door, then held up two bags. "This is an intervention. We brought wine and chocolate since you never keep them in the house."

The heaviness Elise had carried since Dax left returned tenfold. "No chocolate for me. But wine sounds pretty good."

The silence had been deafening. He'd ignored her text messages, even the funny ones. He hadn't called. At first she'd thought it was merely pride, which was why she kept reaching out. But he really didn't want to talk to her.

"Come on, Elise. Live a little. When a man acts like an ass, chocolate is the only cure," Dannie called from the kitchen where she'd gone to fetch wineglasses and a corkscrew.

Tears welled up and the ugly-cry faucet let loose. Dannie flew into the living room and enfolded Elise in a comforting embrace while Juliet looked on helplessly.

Murmuring, Dannie smoothed Elise's hair and let her cry. Sobs wrenched Elise's chest, seizing her lungs until suffocation seemed more likely than a cease-fire of emotions.

Her life had fallen apart. But her friends were here when she needed them.

"It's okay, cry all you want," Dannie suggested. "The endorphins are good for you. It'll help you feel better."

"I know." Dabbing at her eyes ineffectively with a sleeve, Elise sniffled and gave up. "But they don't seem to be working."

"Maybe because Dax is more of an ass than regular men?" Juliet suggested sweetly.

Dannie bit back a snort and Elise choked on an involuntary laugh, which led to a fit of coughing. By the time she recovered, the tears had mostly dried up.

"It wasn't working because it's my fault. I'm the problem, not Dax," Elise confessed.

They might be soul mates, but obviously there was more to it than that. Happily ever after didn't magically happen, and being matched was the beginning of the journey, not the end. And she had no clue how to get where she wanted to be. That's why she couldn't hold on to Dax, no matter how much she loved him.

Everything he'd accused her of was true.

"That's ridiculous." Dannie *tsk*ed.

"I'm not buying that," Juliet said at the same time. "It's always the man's fault."

Elise smiled at the staunch support. She'd had a hand in these two women's becoming the best they could be, in finding happiness with the men they'd married, and it had been enough for so long to be on the sidelines of love, looking in from outside, nose pressed to the glass.

At least then she hadn't known what she was missing.

"Dax has a hard time trusting people," she explained. "I knew that. Yet I didn't tell him we were matched and he took it as a betrayal."

More than a betrayal. She hadn't trusted that he could love the real her. He'd been gradually warming up to the idea of soul mates, putting his faith in her, and she'd forgotten to do the same.

"So what? When you love someone, you forgive

them when they mess up," Juliet declared. "People mess up a lot. It's what makes us human."

"And sometimes, you have to figure out what's best for them, even when they don't know themselves," Dannie advised. "That's part of love, too. Seeing beneath the surface to what a man really wants, instead of what he tells you he wants."

"And sometimes," Elise said quietly, "love isn't enough. Sometimes, you hurt the person you love too much and you can't undo it. That's the lesson here for me."

She'd had a shot at being deliriously in love and ruined it. She'd always believed that if her soul mate existed, then love *would* be enough.

Juliet and Dannie glanced at each other and a long look passed between them.

"You get the wine." Dannie shooed Juliet toward the kitchen and then extracted a jewelry box from her purse.

Juliet returned with the wineglasses, passed them out and perched on the edge of the couch. "Open it, Elise."

After handing the box to Elise, Dannie sat next to Juliet and held her glass of wine in her lap without drinking it.

Carefully, Elise cracked the hinged lid to reveal

a silver necklace. A heart-within-a-heart charm hung from the chain. Surprised, she eyed the two women. "Thank you. But what's this about?"

Dannie unclasped the necklace and drew it around Elise's neck. The cool metal warmed instantly against her skin.

"You gave us necklaces during our makeovers," Dannie said and nodded at Juliet. "We were about to embark on the greatest adventure of our lives. We had your guidance from the first moment we met our matches and it stayed with us every day, right here in silver."

"Open heart." Juliet pointed at Dannie's necklace and then at her own. "Hearts holding each other. Simple but profound messages about love. We wanted to return the favor."

"I had no idea those necklaces meant so much to you." Tears threatened again and Elise blinked them back. "What does mine mean?"

Juliet shook her head with a small smile. "That's for you to figure out at the right time. That's how it works."

"We can't tell you. Just like you didn't tell us." Dannie put a comforting hand on Elise's arm. "I wish I could make it easier for you because honestly, working through the issues I had with Leo was the hardest thing I ever did."

Nodding, Juliet chimed in. "Finn and I are so much alike, it was nearly impossible to compromise. But we found a way and it was so worth it."

Elise fingered the larger heart with the smaller one nestled inside. Her match was a disaster, not like Dannie's and Juliet's. She'd known their matches were solid from the beginning. Of course, it was easier to see such things from the outside.

What was it about matters of your own heart that were so difficult?

That was it. A heart within a heart.

The necklace's meaning came to her on a whisper, growing louder as her consciousness worked through it, embraced it. The large heart was the love between a man and a woman, which had the capacity to be huge and wonderful, eclipsing everything else.

But inside the larger heart lay a smaller heart.

I have to love myself too.

The fat girl inside hadn't vanished when Dax poured chocolate chips over her. Or when he admitted he was falling in love with her. Because it wasn't enough.

She had to be enough, all by herself, with or without a man by her side.

Until she believed she was worthy of loving a man like Dax and allowing him to love her in return, she wasn't his soul mate. She wasn't his perfect match.

Not yet. But she could be.

"I get it. The necklace," Elise clarified, and took the other women's hands in hers, forming a circle. "I know how to get my happily ever after, or at least how to shoot for it. Will you help me?"

"Yes," they said simultaneously.

"You have a plan," Dannie guessed.

Elise nodded slowly as it formed. "Wakefield Media has a box suite at AT&T Stadium, but Dax never goes. He hates the Cowboys." She didn't recall when he'd shared that information. During one of their marathon profile sessions, likely. "But I need him there on Sunday. Can you have Leo make up some reason why they both need to go to a game?"

"Of course." Dannie smiled mischievously. "Leo will do anything I ask. I finally got two pink lines this morning."

"You're pregnant?" Elise gasped as Juliet smiled

and kissed Dannie's cheek. "No wonder you told Juliet to get the wine."

"We're not announcing it. I'm only telling you two because I had to tell *someone*." The glow only made Dannie more beautiful. "But enough about me. I'll get Leo and Dax there."

"Thanks." Elise squeezed both of their hands. "You are the finest ladies I've ever had the privilege of meeting."

The last thing Dax wanted to do was go to a Cowboys game. But Leo insisted and they'd only recently resurrected their friendship. How could he say no and not offend Leo?

Dax would much rather spend the day asleep, but that wasn't an option. He hadn't slept well since that last night with Elise. Spending the day alone held even less appeal. So he went.

The stadium teemed with blue and silver and stars aplenty. The world's fourth-largest high-definition video screen hung from the roof, from the twenty-yard line to the opposing twenty-yard line, and only someone in the media business could fully appreciate the glory of it.

The retractable roof was closed today in deference to the late season weather, which boosted the crowd noise to a new level of loud. Once he and Leo arrived in the luxurious box suite, blessed silence cloaked them both as they ordered beer from the efficient waitstaff and then slid into the high-backed suede stools overlooking the field.

Leo held out his longneck bottle and waited for Dax to clink his to it. They both took a long pull of beer.

After swallowing, Leo said, "Thanks for doing this. I thought we should hang out, just us."

"Sure." Dax shrugged, a little misty himself at the catch in Leo's voice. "No one was using the suite today and the Cowboys are playing the Redskins. It'll be worth it if the 'Skins trounce the homeboys."

The spectacle of the teams taking the field began, and they settled in to watch the game. They sat companionably until halftime, when Leo cleared his throat.

"We've been friends a long time. But some major changes have happened in my life. I've changed. I hope you can respect who I am now and it won't affect our friendship going forward." Leo stared out over the field. "On that note, I have to tell you something. It's huge."

Dax's gut clenched. Leo was about to announce he had two months to live. Or Daniella did.

Fate couldn't be so unkind to such genuine people. And Dax had wasted so much time, time Leo may not have, being stupid and prideful.

"I've been hard on Daniella and on you about her. I'm over it." Over his pettiness, over his inability to be happy for his friend. But not over the slight jealousy that Leo had figured out how to navigate relationship waters with such stellar success. "It's great that you found her. She's amazing and obviously good for you."

"She is. And that's good to hear, because—" Leo grinned and punched Dax on the arm "—I'm going to be a father."

"That's what this bro-date was about?" Dax grinned back as his nerves relaxed. "Congrats. I'm glad if you're glad."

Leo was going to have a family.

Jealousy flared again, brighter, hotter. Shock of all shocks. Dax had never once thought about having a family. Never thought he'd want one. Never dreamed he'd instantly imagine a tiny, beautiful face with dark hair and a sharp wit. A little girl who took after her mother.

"Of course I'm glad! It's the second-best thing

that's happened to me after marrying Dannie." Leo swallowed the last of his beer and set it down with a flourish. "And no. That's not why I insisted we come to the game. That is."

Leo pointed at the jumbo screen in the middle of the stadium. A woman's face filled it. A familiar, dark-haired woman. *Elise.*

Dax's pulse pounded in his throat. "What's going on?"

Audio piped into the suite quite clearly.

"Thanks for giving me thirty seconds, Ed," she said, her voice ringing in Dax's ears, filling the stadium as the crowd murmured and craned their necks to watch. "My name is Elise Arundel and I'm a matchmaker."

What was this all about—advertising? Or much more? He glared at Leo. "You had something to do with this?"

"All her," Leo replied mildly. "I'm just the delivery boy."

Dax's gaze flew back to the screen where Elise was addressing the entire stadium full of Sunday afternoon football fanatics. *Elise* was addressing *80,000 people* voluntarily. If he weren't so raw, he might be proud of her. It must have been difficult for her, given that she didn't like to be the center of attention.

"Some of you saw me on the *Morning Show* a few weeks ago, being interviewed by Dax Wakefield. We struck a deal. If I matched Dax to the love of his life, he'd agree to sing my praises at the Super Bowl. Which is in February and unfortunately, I lost the wager."

Lost? She'd been quite gleeful over the fact that she'd won the last time he'd seen her. His mind kicked into high gear. She was up to something.

"So," she continued. "Congratulations, Dax. You win. You get to put me out of the business of happily ever after. I'm such a good loser, I'm going to let you do it at a football game. All you have to do is join me on camera. Tell these people I didn't change your mind about true love and that you still don't believe soul mates exist."

"How can I do that?" Dax muttered. "I don't know where you are."

"I'm here," Elise said. But in the flesh, not through the stadium's sound system.

He whirled. And there she was, gorgeous and real, and her presence bled through the air, raising heat along his neck. She was within touching distance. He'd missed her, missed her smile, her quirky sense of humor. The way she made him feel.

And then he remembered. She was a liar, a manipulator. She cared only about winning.

Except she'd just announced to 80,000 people that she'd lost. And she'd told him in no uncertain terms that only promoting EA International could get her in front of a camera. Obviously she'd found another motivator, but what?

A cameraman followed her into the suite, lens on Dax. He couldn't even muster a fake grin, let alone his "camera" smile, not when Elise had effectively pinned him to a piece of cork after all. "What is this all about, Elise?"

"I told you. This is your shining moment. It's your chance to ruin me. Go ahead." She nodded to the stadium, where this nightmare was playing out on the screen.

Thousands of eyes were riveted to the drama unfolding and it needed to be over. Now.

He opened his mouth. And closed it. Not only was he pinned to a cork, on display for everyone to examine, she was daring him to lie in public.

He wasn't a liar.

So he didn't lie.

"My soul mate doesn't exist."

Something sharp and wounded glinted in the depths of her eyes.

"Tell them I didn't match you to the love of your life," she suggested clearly, as if the stadium deserved to hear every word regardless of what was going on inside her. "That I'm a fraud and my match software doesn't work."

Obviously, this was not going to end until he gave her what she was asking for.

"True love doesn't exist for me and your match process is flawed," he growled as his pulse spiked and sweat broke out across the back of his heated neck, though both statements were true. "Is that what you wanted me to say?"

It was done. He'd set out to ruin her and now everyone in the stadium, as well as those watching at home, heard him say it. His comments would be broadcast far and wide on social media, he had no doubt.

His stomach churned. The victory was more hollow than his insides.

All at once, he realized why. He'd called off the wager and meant it. But only because he refused to lose and calling it off was the only way to ensure that would never happen.

He and Elise were put together with remarkable

similarity. Was he really going to blame her because she didn't like to lose either?

Leo might have had a small point about Elise bringing her A game.

Too bad the wager was the only real thing they'd ever had between them.

Vulnerability in her expression, she stared at him without blinking. "Is that all? There's nothing more you have to say?"

"I'm done."

Wasn't what he'd already said enough? His heart felt as if it were being squeezed from its mooring through a straw. Did she not realize how painful this was?

She crossed the suite, closing the few yards between them, barging right into his personal space. Finger extended, she pointed right at the area of his torso that hurt the worst.

"You need to tell them the *whole* truth. You not only admitted love does happen to others, you started to believe in it for yourself. In the possibility of soul mates," she said. "Because I matched you with the perfect woman. And you fell in love with her, didn't you?"

He groaned. She'd seen right through his carefully worded statements. Right through him. The curtain didn't exist to her.

He crossed his arms over the ache in his chest. "It would be unfair to say either of us won when in reality, we both lost."

Tenderness and grief welled in her eyes. "Yes. We both lost something precious due to my lack of trust in you. But not because you were untrustworthy. Because I couldn't trust myself, couldn't trust that I was the right person to change your mind about true love. I was convinced you'd end our relationship after a couple of weeks and when I fell in love with you, I—"

"You're in love with me?" Something fluttered in his chest as he searched her face.

All her deepest emotions spilled from her gaze, spreading across her expression, winding through his heart.

It was true.

His pulse spiked and he fought it. What did that really change? Nothing.

"I'm afraid so," she said solemnly. "Nothing but the truth from here on out. I thought love conquered all. But without trust, someone can be perfect for you and still screw it up."

She was talking to him. About him. She knew

he'd let his own issues cloud their relationship, just as she had. He'd let his fears about turning out like his parents taint his life, never giving anyone a chance to betray his trust.

He'd let anger blind him to the truth.

This had never been about winning the wager, for either of them.

"How do you know if you can trust someone forever? That's a long time."

"Fear of the unknown is a particular expertise of mine," she allowed with a small smile. "I like to know what's going to happen, that I can depend on someone. Especially when he promises something so big as to love me for the rest of my life. That's scary. What if he changes his mind? What if—"

"I'm not going to change my mind."

The instant it was out of his mouth, he realized what she'd gotten him to concede. And the significance of it.

"And by the way, same goes," he said. "How do I know you're not going to change yours?"

How had he not seen they were alike even in this? Neither of them trusted easily, yet he'd crucified her over her inability, while tucking his own lack of trust away like a favored treasure. She hadn't been trying to bring him to his knees.

Just trying to navigate something unexpected and making mistakes in the process.

"Let's take it day by day. As long as you're in this relationship fully today, that's the only guarantee I need. I love you." She nodded to the stadium. "I'm not afraid to stand up in front of all these people and tell you how I feel. Are you?"

It was a challenge. A public challenge. If he said he loved her, it would be the equivalent of admitting she'd won. Of admitting she'd done everything she said she would in the interview.

"What are you trying to accomplish here?" he asked.

"I believe this is more commonly known as me calling you on your crap."

Against his will, the corners of his lips turned up. "Is that so?"

Only Elise knew exactly how to do that. Because she got him in a way no one else ever could.

She nodded. "But I had to wade through my own first. When my algorithm matched me with you, it wasn't wrong. But I was. I'm sorry I didn't tell you I was your match. I wasn't ready to trust you. I am now."

And she'd proved it by declaring her flaws to the world on the big screen, publicly. The one place she said she'd go only for her business. But she'd done it for him because *he* was her motivator. Because she loved him.

Somehow, that made it easier to confess his own sins.

"I…messed up, too. I wasn't about to stick around and find out I couldn't trust you to stay, so I didn't. I'm sorry I didn't give you that chance."

The exact accusation he'd flung at her. His relationship philosophy might as well be Do Unto Others Before They Do Unto You. That ended today. If he loved Elise and knew beyond a doubt he wasn't going to change his mind, he wasn't broken. Just incomplete.

His soul needed a mate to be whole.

Her smile belied the sudden tears falling onto her cheeks. "You didn't meet your soul mate because your soul mate wasn't ready to meet you. But I am ready now." She held out her hand as if they'd just been introduced for the first time. "My name is Shannon Elise Arundel, but you can call me Elise."

He didn't hesitate but immediately grasped her fingers and yanked her into a kiss. As his mouth met hers and fused, his heart opened up and out spilled the purest form of happiness.

He'd found his soul mate, and it turned out he didn't want a woman who didn't care what was behind his curtain. He wanted this woman, who'd invited herself backstage and taken up residence in the exact spot where she belonged.

She'd been one step ahead of him the entire time. She was the only woman alive who could outthink, outsmart and out-love him.

Lifting his head slightly, he murmured against her lips, "I love you too. And for the record, I'd rather call you mine."

An "aww" went up from the spectators and without taking his attention off the woman in his arms, Dax reached out to cover the lens with his palm. Some things weren't meant to be televised.

Epilogue

Elise's first Super Bowl party was in full swing and surprisingly, she'd loved every minute of it. It had been her idea and Dax let her plan the whole thing. And he didn't mind that she spent more time in the kitchen with Dannie and a host of female guests cooing over baby talk now that Dannie was in her second trimester.

"Hon," Dax called from the living room. "I think you'd better come see this."

Immediately, Elise set down her wine and moved to comply. The other women snickered but that didn't slow her down.

"What?" she called over her shoulder. "If any of you had a gorgeous man like that in your bed every night, you'd jump when he said jump, too."

She sailed out of the kitchen to join Dax on the couch in front of the sixty-five-inch LED TV that now dominated her—their—living room. It was the only thing Dax had requested they keep from his loft when he moved in with her at Christmas.

How could she say no? They hardly ever watched it anyway. Neither football nor science fiction movies held a candle to doing everything together—going to the grocery store, dinner and sometimes even to work with each other. It was heaven on earth and it could not possibly get any better.

"I like what I see so far," she told him as her gaze lit on his beautiful face.

Dax grinned and took her hand, nodding at the TV. "You can look at me anytime. That's what you should be focusing on."

The game had cut to a commercial break. A Coca-Cola polar bear faded away as one commercial ended and another began. A familiar logo materialized on the screen. *Her* logo. EA International's, to be precise.

"What did you do?" she sputtered around a startled laugh.

"I owed you the match fee. Watch," Dax advised her and she did, fingers to her numb lips.

A montage of clips from her confessional at the

Cowboys game flashed, interspersed with snippets of former clients espousing her praises in five-second sound bites. The whole commercial was cleverly edited to allow Elise's speech about true love to play out in real time in the form of happy couples. Then the last scene snapped into focus and it was Dax.

"EA International specializes in soul mates," the digital version of Dax said sincerely, his charisma so crisp and dazzling on the sixty-five-inch screen she nearly wept. "That's where I found mine. Elise, I love you. Will you marry me?"

Her pulse stopped, but her brain kept going, echoing with the sound of Dax's smooth voice.

The screen faded to a car commercial and the house full of people went dead silent as Dax dropped to his knees in front of her, his expression earnest. "I'm sorry, but I can't call you Ms. Arundel any longer."

And then he winked, setting her heart in motion again as she laughed through the tears that had sprung up after all. "You can call me Mrs. Wakefield. I insist."

Applause broke out and Elise was gratified to feel absolutely no heat in her cheeks. Dax lived in the spotlight, and she'd deal with it gladly because she wanted to stand next to him for the rest of her life.

The crowd shifted their attention to other things, leaving Dax and Elise blessedly alone. Or at least as alone as they could be with thirty people in the house.

Without a lot of fanfare, Dax pulled a box out of his pocket and produced a beautiful, shiny diamond ring, eclipsed only by the wattage of his smile. "I'm assuming that's a yes."

She nodded, shaking loose a couple of the tears. "Though I'm intrigued to find out what you'd planned as a backup to that commercial if I said no."

How could he come up with anything more effective than *that?* He'd declared his love for her, asked her to marry him and endorsed her business in the most inarguable way possible. He was brilliant and all hers.

It was better than a fairy tale. Better than Cinderella because he saw *her*, the real her, underneath. No makeover, no fancy dresses. If she gained a few pounds, he wouldn't care.

"No backup," he said smugly and slipped the ring on her finger, which fit precisely right, of course. Dax Wakefield never missed a trick. "I knew you'd say yes since I proposed during the Super Bowl. You know, because it's less predictable than Valentine's Day."

Her heart caught on an erratic, crazy beat. He remembered what she'd said on that park bench a season ago. That alone made him her perfect match. The rest was icing on the cake.

"I thought being with you couldn't get any better. How like you to prove me wrong," she teased and then sobered, taking his jaw between both of hands. His ring winked back at her from its place on her third finger, perfect and right. "Don't stop, even if I tell you to, okay?"

"Deal." He leaned forward to kiss her sweetly, and against her lips, mouthed, "I love you."

"I love you, too."

Happily ever after had finally arrived. For both of them.

* * * * *

MILLS & BOON®

Why shop at millsandboon.co.uk?

Each year, thousands of romance readers find their perfect read at millsandboon.co.uk. That's because we're passionate about bringing you the very best romantic fiction. Here are some of the advantages of shopping at www.millsandboon.co.uk:

✴ **Get new books first**—you'll be able to buy your favourite books one month before they hit the shops

✴ **Get exclusive discounts**—you'll also be able to buy our specially created monthly collections, with up to 50% off the RRP

✴ **Find your favourite authors**—latest news, interviews and new releases for all your favourite authors and series on our website, plus ideas for what to try next

✴ **Join in**—once you've bought your favourite books, don't forget to register with us to rate, review and join in the discussions

Visit **www.millsandboon.co.uk**
for all this and more today!

ANGEL OF THE EVENING

Brie Roberts is about to start a new job, as companion to a young girl on the island of Corfu, when her roommate, Claire, invites her to a science fiction convention. Deserted by Claire she 'bumps' into Adam Andrikos, handsome TV tycoon who happens to be the half-brother of her new charge and therefore her boss. Linked together romantically by the newspapers, after hints from Adam, Brie takes up her new post with a sense of foreboding.

ANGEL OF THE EVENING